T0115302

THE ETERNAL
ONES OF THE
DREAM

THE ETERNAL ONES OF THE DREAM

SELECTED POEMS
1990–2010

JAMES TATE

ecco

AN *IMPRINT OF* HARPERCOLLINS*PUBLISHERS*

THE ETERNAL ONES OF THE DREAM. Copyright © 2012 by James Tate. All rights reserved. Printed in the United States of America. No part of this book may be used or reproduced in any manner whatsoever without written permission except in the case of brief quotations embodied in critical articles and reviews. For information address HarperCollins Publishers, 195 Broadway, New York, NY 10007.

HarperCollins books may be purchased for educational, business, or sales promotional use. For information please e-mail the Special Markets Department at SPsales@harpercollins.com.

FIRST EDITION

Designed by Mary Austin Speaker

Library of Congress Cataloging-in-Publication Data has been applied for.

ISBN 978-0-06-210186-0

22 23 24 25 26 LBC 11 10 9 8 7

FOR DARA,
FOR EMILY
AND GUY

CONTENTS

SHROUD OF THE GNOME

MEMOIR OF THE HAWK

RETURN TO THE CITY
OF WHITE DONKEYS

THE GHOST SOLDIERS

ACKNOWLEDGMENTS

Agni, the *American Poetry Review, Antaeus, Bellevue Literary Review*, the Best of the Prose Poem, *Boston Review, Both, Boulevard, Caliban, canwehaveourballback, Colorado Review, Conduit, Conjunctions, Crab Orchard Review, Crazyhorse, Crowd, Cue, Cut Bank, Denver Quarterly, Erewon, Fence, Field*, the *Germ*, the *Gettysburg Review, Grand Street, Green Mountain Review, Harvard Book Review, Harvard Review*, the *Hollins Critic, Hunger Mountain*, the *Iowa Review, jubilat, Lit*, the *Massachusetts Review*, the *Mississippi Review*, the *Missouri Review*, the *Nation, New American Writing, New England Quarterly, New Letters*, the *New Republic*, the *New York Times*, the *New Yorker, Ontario Review, Orbis, P. N. Magazine, Painted Bride Quarterly*, the *Paris Review, Partisan Review, Pequod, Pleiades, Ploughshares, Poetry*, Poetry Center of Chicago, *Poetry International, Poets & Writers, Prairie Schooner, Prose Poem International, Quick Fictions, Raritan*, Sarabande Books, *Southern California Anthology*, the *Threepenny Review, Tin House, TriQuarterly, Verse*, the *Village Voice, Virginia Quarterly Review, Volt, Washington Square Review*, the *Yale Review*.

THE ETERNAL
ONES OF THE
DREAM

DISTANCE FROM
LOVED ONES

Quabbin Reservoir

All morning, skipping stones on the creamy lake,
I thought I heard a lute being played, high up,
in the birch trees, or a faun speaking French
with a Brooklyn accent. A snowy owl watched me
with half-closed eyes. "What have you done for me
philately," I wanted to ask, licking the air.
There was a village at the bottom of the lake,
and I could just make out the old post office,
and, occasionally, when the light struck it just right,
I glimpsed several mailmen swimming in or out of it,
letters and packages escaping randomly, 1938, 1937,
it didn't matter to them any longer. *Void.*
No such address. Soft blazes squirmed across the surface
and I could see their church, now home to druid squatters,
rock in the intoxicating current, as if to an ancient hymn.
And a thousand elbowing reeds conducted the drowsy band pavilion:
awake, awake, you germs of habit! Alas, I fling
my final stone, my calling card, my gift of porphyry
to the citizens of the deep, and disappear into a copse,
raving like a butterfly to a rosebud: I love you.

Peggy in the Twilight

Peggy spent half of each day trying to wake up, and
the other half preparing for sleep. Around five, she
would mix herself something preposterous and '40s-ish
like a Grasshopper or a Brass Monkey, adding a note
of gaiety to her defeat. This shadowlife became her.
She always had a glow on; that is, she carried an aura
of innocence as well as death with her.

  I first met her at a party almost thirty years ago.
Even then it was too late for tragic women, tragic
anything. Still, when she was curled up and fell asleep
in the corner, I was overwhelmed with feelings of love.
Petite black and gold angels sat on her slumped shoulders
and sang lullabies to her.

  I walked into another room and asked our host for
a blanket for Peggy.

  "Peggy?" he said. "There's no one here by that name."

  And so my lovelife began.

Distance from Loved Ones

After her husband died, Zita decided to get the face-lift
she had always wanted. Halfway through the operation
her blood pressure started to drop, and they had to stop.
When Zita tried to fasten her seat belt for her sad drive
home, she threw out her shoulder. Back at the hospital
the doctor examined her and found cancer run rampant
throughout her shoulder and arm and elsewhere. Radiation
followed. And, now, Zita just sits there in her beauty parlor,
bald, crying and crying.

My mother tells me all this on the phone, and I say:
Mother, who is Zita?

And my mother says, I am Zita. All my life I have been
Zita, bald and crying. And you, my son, who should have known
me best, thought I was nothing but your mother.

But, Mother, I say, I am dying. . . .

Bewitched

I was standing in the lobby,
some irritant in my eye,
thinking back on a soloist
I once heard in Venezuela,
and then, for some reason,
on a crate of oranges recently
arrived from a friend in Florida,
and then this colleague came up to me
and asked me what time it was,
and I don't know what came over me
but I was certain that I was standing there naked
and I was certain she could see my thoughts,
so I tried to hide them quickly,
I was embarrassed that there was
no apparent connection to them,
will-o'-the-wisps, and I needed an alibi,
so I told her I had seen a snapshot
of a murder victim recently
that greatly resembled her,
and that she should take precaution,
my intonation getting me into deeper trouble,
and I circled the little space I had cut out
as if looking for all the sidereal years
she had inquired into moments before,
and the dazzling lunar poverty of some thoughts
had me pinned like a moth
and my dubious tactic to hide my malady
had prompted this surreptitious link

to the whirling Sufi dancers,

once so popular in these halls.

"It's five minutes past four," I said,

knowing I had perjured myself for all time.

I veered into the men's room,

astonished to have prevailed,

my necktie, a malediction stapled in place,

my zipper synchronized with the feminine motive.

In Zagreb, just now, a hunter is poaching some cherries.

Saturdays Are for Bathing Betsy

I am thinking about Betsy almost all the time now.
I am also thinking about the relationship between
a man and his watch. I am amazed at how each sort
of animal and plant manages to keep its kind alive.
Shocking poultry. Maybe there's a movie playing
downtown about a dotty fat woman with a long knife
who dismembers innocent ducks and chickens. But it
is the reconstruction of the villa of the mysteries
that is killing me. How each sort of animal and
plant prevents itself from returning to dust
just a little while longer while I transfer some
assets to a region where there are no thinking creatures,
just worshipping ones. They oscillate along like magicians,
deranged seaweed fellows and their gals, a Nile landscape
littered with Pygmies. I'm lolling on the banks.
I am not just a bunch of white stuff inside my skull.
No, there is this villa, and in the villa there is
a bathing pool, and on Saturdays Betsy always visits.
I am not the first rational man, but my tongue
does resemble a transmitter. And, when wet, she
is a triangle. And when she's wet, time has a fluff-
iness about it, and that has me trotting about,
loathing any locomotion not yoked to her own.

How Happy We Were

There was a spy in my life who wouldn't let me sleep.
Day in and day out she tortured me with the most sophisticated
devices. At first I squealed like a pig at slaughter.
Then I became addicted. Between sessions I was agitated
and impatient. I cried, "How much longer must I wait?"
So she made me wait longer and longer. I became masterful,
a genius of the thumbscrew and rack. I didn't really need her
any longer. On her last visit she could read this in my eyes,
and it tore a hole in her through which I could see
something like eternity and a few of the little angels
whose sole job it is to fake weeping for people like us.

Consolations After an Affair

My plants are whispering to one another:

they are planning a little party

later on in the week about watering time.

I have quilts on beds and walls

that think it is still the 19th century.

They know nothing of automobiles and jet planes.

For them a wheat field in January

is their mother and enough.

I've discovered that I don't need

a retirement plan, a plan to succeed.

A snow leopard sleeps beside me

like a slow, warm breeze.

And I can hear the inner birds singing

alone in this house I love.

"Burn Down the Town, No Survivors"

Those were my orders,
issued with a sense of rightness
I'd rarely known. I was tired
of how June was treating John,
how Mary was victimizing herself
with nearly everyone, Mark
was a loose cannon, and Carlotta
would never find any peace.
It seemed to me that there could be
no acceptable resolution for anyone,
except those who didn't deserve one.
And when, for a moment, I held the power,
I surveyed the landscape—it was
just a typical mid-sized town
in the middle of nowhere—and
the citizens showed no signs
of remorse, as if what they were doing
to one another (and to me) was
what we were here for (and I recognize
the mistake in that kind of thinking,
but still . . .) a bold and decisive action
seemed so appealing, even healing.
I was with a friend's wife, her
wild mane would make such ideal kindling—
I could have loved her but it would
have been just more of the same,
more petty crimes and slow death,
more passion leading to betrayal,

more ecstasy guaranteeing tears. I saw
how dangerous and fragile I had become.
I could have loved a fig right then
with my gasoline in one hand,
and the other fluttering between
her breast and a packet of matches.
My contagious laughter frightening us both,
"No survivors," I repeated, and
we looked through one another,
the work already completed.

Under Mounting Pressure

"O Marcel," she says to me, "O Marcel,

do you know the way out of this pool?

I am very tired of swimming about here."

A gale from her shoulder left me in dishabille.

I was in dishabille anyway as I was just back

from the kaleidoscopic society.

I was just there to salute her as she passed.

She was a floating beautyfarm.

I had planned to escort her to the demolition derby.

She was a floating beautyfarm

and I stood there on the wharf of the final landing.

She recognized me as some Marcel-type of guy—

this was incomprehensible to me, but preparatory

to something perhaps worthwhile.

A quizzical, if concupiscent smile exhausted itself in my head

and I stretched out my hand, the Grand Mogul I really was.

I started reeling in this wildcat beautyfarm,

it was a big one. Her ledger of love was a blur,

her helmet was full of holes. "O Marcel," she said to me,

"O Marcel, there's a doorbell in your head. Don't touch it!"

Certain Nuances, Certain Gestures

                              The way a lady
entertaining an illicit desire touches her earlobe
in a crowded room, and the way that room seems to single
her out and undress her with murmuring torchlight—
if the right spectator is present, even though the
band is playing loudly and the myriad celebrants
are toasting their near-tragic rise to glory, and the
Vice President of an important bank is considering
an assassination, and even the mice in the boiler room
are planning a raid on an old bag of cookies in the
attic—even so, this spectator senses the moisture
on her palms, can feel her thoughts wander in and out
of the cavernous room; knows, too, their approximate
destination. Beyond this, he refuses to follow.
She stands alone there on the quay, waiting. The
river of life is flowing. The spectator returns
to his room, a few hours closer to his own death
or ecstasy. He makes a few hasty entries into his
diary before turning off the light. And, yes, he dreams,
but of a gazelle frozen in the path of a runaway truck.

Trying to Help

On another planet, a silvery starlet is brooding
on her salary. Some gangling ranchers are blindfolding her
for her own good, or so they say. It's all part of some lawful
research, or maybe they said "awful research," I wasn't listening.
I was roving down a chestnut lane, thinking about origins
in a contrite sort of way, amid the nearly inaudible society
of aphids and such, modulating my little hireling feet
none too carefully, an average stroller praying for keepsakes,
or at least one, when I heard this eerie squeak from afar.
For reasons which I refuse to explain I knew instantly
what was going on, and I tried to negotiate in my rudimentary way.
I offered up some rose petals, I think they were tempted
but liked playing tough because it was in their contract
or something. So I offered to play the fiddle on their patio
for a whole night. No deal—I don't think they knew what a fiddle was,
which was actually lucky for me since I have but one tiny tune.
I sat down on my chestnut lane, tempted to sneer at my own timidity.
Those squeaks from afar, all that damned distant research,
provide the only keepsake for this day, my momentum crushed.
Hours pass, crows pass, a pheasant crashes into an oak tree.
In a dream she says to me, "Thanks for caring, mister,
but it's all part of the plot, and I'm getting paid awfully well."
And now I can hardly walk.

Ebb

A mountaineer and a dentist were placing cheesecloth
over their thing. It was frosty out, though they both
were sleeveless. I was thumbing through my stamp album,
sipping something smooth on my ancient mattress, something
greenish, dabbling at psychic research, fingering
my harmonica, remembering a few Psalm fragments.
The dentist was looking doubtfully at a handful of chunky
crystals—I think he is an orphan—I saw him in a newsreel
during the long summer of '58; he hands them to the mountaineer—
who feels invaded, motherless. And there could be a windstorm
coming any minute now, I feel its electricity rising in my veins.
All of us will be completely varnished, I mean drenched.
The wagons should be closing, we should be cooperating.
It is impossible to duplicate the pot roast I had before leaving.
We are completely exposed, like a rabbi facing a stork—
I mean, there's this inanimate thinness in the tremors,
and the bestowing of the crystals makes me want to cry
as if I myself had thrown a pet goose out the porthole
just as the situation, usually so diverting, was now
ushering in the dismaying, leprous, sustained smallness
prayed for but forgotten in our grandfather's last days.

I Am a Finn

I am standing in the post office, about
to mail a package back to Minnesota, to my family.
I am a Finn. My name is Kasteheimi (Dewdrop).

Mikael Agricola (1510–1557) created the Finnish language.
He knew Luther and translated the New Testament.
When I stop by the Classé Café for a cheeseburger

no one suspects that I am a Finn.
I gaze at the dimestore reproductions of Lautrec
on the greasy walls, at the punk lovers afraid

to show their quivery emotions, secure
in the knowledge that my grandparents really did
emigrate from Finland in 1910—why

is everyone leaving Finland, hundreds of
thousands to Michigan and Minnesota, and now Australia?
Eighty-six percent of Finnish men have blue

or grey eyes. Today is Charlie Chaplin's
one hundredth birthday, though he is not
Finnish or alive: "Thy blossom, in the bud

laid low." The commonest fur-bearing animals
are the red squirrel, muskrat, pine marten
and fox. There are about 35,000 elk.

But I should be studying for my exam.

I wonder if Dean will celebrate with me tonight,

assuming I pass. Finnish literature

really came alive in the 1860s.

Here, in Cambridge, Massachusetts,

no one cares that I am a Finn.

They've never even heard of Frans Eemil Sillanpää,

winner of the 1939 Nobel Prize in Literature.

As a Finn, this infuriates me.

I Am Still a Finn

I failed my exam, which is difficult
for me to understand because I am a Finn.
We are a bright, if slightly depressed, people.

Pertti Palmroth is the strongest name
in Finnish footwear design; his shoes and boots
are exported to seventeen countries.

Dean brought champagne to celebrate
my failure. He says I was just nervous.
Between 1908 and 1950, 33 volumes

of The Ancient Poetry of the Finnish People
were issued, the largest work of its kind
ever published in any language.

So why should I be nervous? Aren't I
a Finn, descendant of Johan Ludvig Runeberg
(1804–1877), Finnish National poet?

I know he wrote in Swedish, and this
depresses me still. Harvard Square
is never "empty." There is no chance

that I will ever be able to state honestly
that "Harvard Square is empty tonight."
A man from Nigeria will be opening

his umbrella, and a girl from Wyoming
will be closing hers. A Zulu warrior
is running to catch a bus and an over-

painted harlot from Buenos Aires will
be fainting on schedule. And I, a Finn,
will long for the dwarf birches of the north

I have never seen. For 73 days the sun
never sinks below the horizon. O
darkness, mine! I shall always be a Finn.

The Expert

talks on and on.
At times he seems lost
in his own personal references,
to be adrift in a lonely pleasure craft.
He has spent his life collecting evidence,
and now it is oozing away down the aisles
of indifferent eavesdroppers.
He spins and points out the window:
"There," he says passionately,
"that is what I mean."
We look: a squirrel flicks its tail and disappears.
His point made, the expert yawns
and we can see deep into his cavernous body.
We are impressed, but also frightened
because there appears to be a campfire
almost out of control on the left bank
of his cave. But then he is off
on one of his special obsessions
and we are back to feeling inferior
and almost nonexistent. We have never
even heard of this phenomenon:
how a thing can hurt and still
grow that fast until it walks off
the map and keep growing while
falling through space. We want
to pinch ourselves, but softly
and slowly. Who among us
invited this expert? He is pacing now

as though flirting with some edge
only he can see. Someone shouts
"Jump!" and he wakes again
and eyes us with suspicion,
and maybe we are guilty of something.
We have no idea what he has given
his life for, though I think
it has something to do with
a monster under the bed.
He is growing old before our eyes,
and no one can catch him now,
no one, that is, except his lost mother.

Poem

The angel kissed my alphabet,
it tingled like a cobweb in starlight.
A few letters detached themselves
and drifted in shadows, a loneliness
they carry like infinitesimal coffins
on their heads.

She kisses my alphabet
and a door opens: blackbirds roosting
on far ridges. A windowpeeper
under an umbrella watches
a funeral service. Blinkered horses
drum the cobblestones.

She kisses: Plunderers gather
in a lackluster ballroom
to display their booty. Mice
testify against one another
in dank rodent courtrooms.

The angel kisses my alphabet,
she squeezes and bites,
and the last lights flutter,
and the violins are demented.
Moisture spreads across my pillow,
a chunk of quartz thirsts
to abandon my brain trust.

Taxidermy

The pastel bees I found in my mattress
really belong to the gravedigger. I was swallowing
my pencil down at headquarters when a meat loaf
crept out of the encyclopedia; it was shaped
like a chicken wearing a tiara but sinking in quicksand.
I hate this job, it's murder. The profile of a horse,
even a champion, can get rabbity, if the knitting needle
slips just a little. Thereupon my tranquilizer takes effect
and wrinkles disappear as if on a sailboat,
a twelve-inch one, and waterspouts bicycle around
like rodents plowing trenches, their equipment
concealed at night under the stairwell.
I'm all thumbs now. I get pregnant
squeezing my thumbs through buttonholes.
I'd like an atrocity to happen
just so I could enjoy the autumnal spice.
Everything is dead anyway, this mouse.
The squad on the beach stuffs my laundress.
Hitherto, the cameras of perdition crackling
as at an auction: How much for that one?
Will it last my lifetime?
Will it fade?

WORSHIPFUL COMPANY OF FLETCHERS

Go, Youth

I was in a dreamstate and this was causing a problem
with the traffic. I felt lonely, like I'd missed the boat,
or I'd found the boat and it was deserted. In the middle
of the road a child's shoe glistened. I walked around it.
It woke me up a little. The child had disappeared. Some
mysteries are better left alone. Others are dreary, distasteful,
and can disarrange a shadow into a thing of unspeakable beauty.
Whose child is that?

What a Patient Does

I follow the tinkle of the lead llama's bell,

a shadow in the memory of man, while maintaining

a strict radio silence. I could see a Chieftain

on a hill surveying ancient ruins.

The breath of leaves and moss and green daylight,

a stray pig snapping at his ankles.

From the tar pit of the obvious I did nothing.

I maintained a strict radio silence, humming.

Flocks of beetles settled on the leaves of tangerine trees.

A tiny ladybird beetle dreamed I was its loyal ally.

To my right is a man reading on a rock.

He thinks he has renounced the world, but there he is,

occupying a little space. An empty chair beside him

has another idea. It is rocking to and fro.

I tell myself: I'll move like water over this undergrowth.

And then I draw back and hold my breath. Something

I've never seen before: a pig breaking in two.

Fingers of lightning flash. The llama looks

very much like a sheep with a long neck. Its head

is a cloud of dust and gas located among the stars.

Autosuggestion: USS North Carolina

And that is the largest battleship in the world, I said.
And see how small it really is. Isn't that encouraging?
She pointed her head toward the drinking fountain,
but was having none of it. A dog from the mental ward
hopped over her. We had driven all the way to Surf City
for some peace and it's not as though it eluded us
so much as it did circle us. The pelicans were on display.
They did pelican-like dives into the surf and came up
wanting bit parts in a movie other than ours.
We were surprisingly graceful and called Pest Control.
That whole day was like a dream leaking into our satchel.
It was stained permanently, but so attractive
we couldn't have designed it better, and we knew nothing
about design. The battleship seemed stalled forever,
or it was a little intimidated by its own reputation.
Whatever the case, we held the idea of a torpedo
gingerly in our minds and meandered without launching it.
Most of the natives were under house arrest.
They wore ankle bracelets and watched us from their windows
or monitors. We couldn't go any farther than this.
We were touring our Armed Forces here and there.
Some of the ammo felt moldy. The officers, though,
were made of steel, soft and pliable,
like stuffed animals. They wet their beds—that seemed
to be the unifying principle. But what did we know?
We were rank amateurs. We were poseurs of the worst sort.
We were out of our league. We belonged in Little League
uniforms, but we couldn't afford them, and our sponsors

were idiots and dunces and drifters and no-count
amalgamated mud merchants. This left us free of debt
and free of riches, which can be so heavy to transport.
We were airy and free and broke and lost
figure skaters or trigger fish, whatever.
And whenever one of the ships felt like sinking
we just picked up magazines and pretended to read
about something else, like a migraine headache
discovered still pounding inside a 10,000-year-old
snowman holding up the North Pole. Incredible! we'd say.
And, who could believe in that? 35,000 tons of history,
going, going—so long. Next, we are going to visit
planets of the solar system, like Burma and Senegal.
But the Department of Housing and Urban Development
says there is heartache and neuralgia starting to blossom there,
but also hydroponics is being discovered.
We have decided to travel by hydroplane,
though, sadly, there is no water anywhere as yet.

A Missed Opportunity

A word sits on the kitchen counter
next to the pitcher of cream
with its blue cornflowers bent.
Perhaps a guest left it in a hurry
or as a tip for good service,
or as a fist against some imagined
insult. Or it fell with some old
plaster from the ceiling, a word
some antediluvian helpmate
hushed up. It picked itself up
from the floor, brushed itself off
and, somehow, scratched its way
up the cupboards. It appears to be
a word of considerable strength
and even significance, but I can't
bring myself to look into its gaze.
The cornflowers are pointing toward
the cookies not far away. An expert
could be called to defuse the word,
but it is Sunday and they are still
sleeping or singing, and, besides that,
the word seems to have moved again
on its own, and now it appears warm
and welcoming, it throbs with life
and a sincere desire to understand me.
It looks slightly puzzled and hurt,

as though I . . . I take a step toward it,
I hold out my hand. "Friend," I say,
but it is shrinking, it is going away
to its old home in the familiar
cold dark of the human parking lot.

50 Views of Tokyo

Only flyspecks remain.
I have not a thought in my head.
My head is a giant pumpkin with a thousand legs.
That must be the elusive thought I was after.
I am feeling a degree of relief and even confidence
after that exercise. Now I remember December 22, 1935.
A bunch of young officers, including yours truly,
met in a restaurant in Shinjuku to discuss a plot.
That's all I remember. The communal spirit
of the valley drifted away. Maybe it was sad.
Then again it might have been a great joke.
I was going to publish *A Secret History,*
but I lost it or it got stolen, perhaps in a subway.
These days I relish a second opinion.
Could there have been another, a better war?
I think I was the one who ran away, who climbed a tree
and then another tree, and then the last one.
I was suffering from postnatal insanity.
I ran into the Matsuya Department Store and said
to the pretty young salesgirl, "Your papa and I
thank you from the bottom of our hearts!"
She started to giggle, and then a few tears eked out
and I sat down on the floor exhausted.
It felt like 1945, like everything was finished.
I remember at some point I had leeches on my face.
An American soldier offered to remove them.
I thought, it's too soon to harvest them,
they'll get much bigger. The Hotel Kaijo was occupied.

I was wishing I could sit on top
of The Five Storied pagoda in Ueno Park
as in the first days when I had no thoughts.
Once I sat on the toilet in the lobby
of the wrestling amphitheater for several hours
astonished that this was my life, my only life,
and I had nothing better to do than sit there.
I didn't care even a little bit about wrestling
and I thought that made me some kind of freakish monster.
If someone had walked in on me and said, "Excuse me,
but would you like to join me for some wakame seaweed from Naruto
cooked with new bamboo shoots and leaf buds?
Perhaps we can solve a few of those riddles
so troubling to young persons like yourself,"
I might have bitten his nose. I was a wild animal
without a soul or a home or a name.
And now I see it wasn't a stage I was going through.
That stage, that stageless stage, was my home
and my name and my soul, and the maze of years
and the endless palaver, the well-wishing
like a blue smoke circling, the world-order
tilting this way and that, the extinct species
coming back to haunt, the rice birds and the butterflies
circling and disappearing, O I longed for one firm
handshake and a kick in the butt I could understand.
A terribly pretty snake stared into my one good eye
and I said this is something I can understand.
After a while I hung it from my neck

and went waltzing with the devil on Asakusa Show Street.

That's when we dreamed up the war to kill

this boredom and its hallowed tradition of proscribed behavior.

Soon everyone would be hanging themselves from the gaslights

and cackling with otherworldly delight.

A child played a lute with such purity of sound

streetcars stopped to applaud.

And a horse made a speech praising the damned.

These are my memories, a white Navy Hospital,

a kiss outside the British Embassy.

What the City Was Like

The city was full of blue devils,
and, once, during an eclipse, the river
began to glow, and a small body walked out of it
carrying a wooden ship full of vegetables
which we mistook for pearls.
We made necklaces of them, and tiaras and bracelets,
and the small body laughed until
its head fell off, and soon enough we realized
our mistake, and grew weak with our knowledge.
Across town, a man lived his entire life
without ever going out on the street.
He destroyed his part of the city many times
without getting off his sofa.
But that neighborhood has always blossomed afresh.
Pixies germinated in the still pools under streetlights.
Cattle grazed in back of the bakery
and helped deliver baked goods to the needy.
A mouse issued commands in a benevolent, judicious, and cheerful manner.
A small, headless body lay in the road,
and passersby clicked their heels.
Across the street the Military Academy
had many historic spots on its windows,
thanks, in part, to the rivers and canals
which carried large quantities of freight
into the treasure house of maps
and music scores necessary for each war.
The spots were all given names by the janitors—
River of Unwavering Desire, River of Untruth,

Spring of Spies, Rill of Good Enough Hotelkeepers,

and then, of course, there was the Spot of Spots.

Nobody paid any attention to the wars,

though there must have been a few or more.

The citizens of the city were wanderers

who did not live in any one place

but roamed the boulevards and alleyways

picking up gum wrappers and setting them down again.

We were relieved when modern ice skating

was finally invented: the nuns glided in circles

for days on end, and this was the greatest blessing.

Behind City Hall salt was mined

under a powerful magnifying glass,

and each grain was tasted by someone

named Mildred until she became a stenographer

and moved away, and no one could read

her diacritical remarks, except the little devils.

For years Mildred sent cards at Christmas,

and then nothing, and no one said a thing.

The city was covered with mountains

which ran straight down the center,

and on the southern tip there were several

volcanoes which could erupt on demand.

Or so it was said, though no one demanded proof.

It was a sketchy little volcano of normal girth

where Dolley Madison hosted her parties

more often than I care to remember.

She served ice cream when she was coming.

She came early and stayed late, as they say,

until all the lights were off and the guests

had lost all hope of regaining their senses.

It is not certain if she possessed a cupcake at that time.

She might have had one in her cellar

as no one was allowed to penetrate her there.

And then the prairie dogs arrived

and caused incorrect pips to appear

on the radar screen, for which they became famous,

and which precipitated the rapid decline

of the Know-Nothings—not a minute too soon.

In the days that followed children were always screaming.

You could set their hair on fire and, sure enough,

they'd start screaming.

The Great Root System

When the birds talk, I answer.
When they are hungry, I need feed.
They desire to propagate, I do too.
But the story ends here, it goes
nowhere. It's just too early
in the morning to think anything through.
A thought starts up, it's like tickling
in my brain. My motor's running
but I'm almost out of gas.
I look at my appointment calendar—
spiderwebs and chicken scratches.
Ah, I see, there's a ladybug coming tomorrow.
For a block of wood, I am so very busy.
I am waiting for the phone to ring.
Is that you, Tweetie? Not a peep.
I flick on the television: no news
is still no news. It's *terribly* early.
It's not as though I have a cow to milk,
or do I? A lovely bovine ruminant
would provide such satisfaction
at this moment. Or a cowbird—
amazing to think of the cowbird
because it makes no nest, and lays
its eggs in the nests of other birds.
What a concept! And, usually, the foster parents—
listen to me! I'm talking of birds
as foster parents, this is really fun—
do not seem to notice anything strange

about the young cowbird, which may be
twice the size of their own chicks.
(This thought has completely exhausted me,
I'm seriously considering a return
to the dark—but safe—underbelly of sleep.)
My own humanity has overwhelmed me,
it has nearly defeated me, the me who was
trying to rise up. It—that is, my own
humanity—seethed up when I least wanted it.
Following the magnetic forces of other worlds,
the birds fly in all directions,
less bird-like than myself.

Loyalty

This is the hardest part:
when I came back to life
I was a good family dog
and not too friendly with strangers.
I got a thirty-five dollar raise
in salary, and through the pea-soup fogs
I drove the General, and introduced him
at rallies. I had a totalitarian approach
and was a massive boost to his popularity.
I did my best to reduce the number of people.
The local bourgeoisie did not exist.
One of them was a mystic
and walked right over me
as if I were a bed of hot coals.
This is par for the course—
I will be employing sundry golf metaphors
henceforth, because a dog, best friend
and chief advisor to the General, should.
While dining with the General I said,
"Let's play the back nine in a sacred rage.
Let's tee off over the foredoomed community
and putt ourselves thunderously, touching bottom."
He drank it all in, rugged and dusky.
I think I know what he was thinking.
He held his automatic to my little head
and recited a poem about my many weaknesses,
for which I loved him so.

Little Poem with Argyle Socks

Behind every great man
there sits a rat.
And behind every great rat,
there's a flea.
Beside the flea there is an encyclopedia.
Every now and then the flea sneezes, looks up,
and flies into action, reorganizing history.
The rat says, "God, I *hate* irony."
To which the great man replies,
"Now now now, darling, drink your tea."

A Manual of Enlargement

Early on
I did some hopeful scratching
in my garden patch.
I saw green!
It's really nice this time.
It's beginning to seem like
a plausible life.
It's Presidents' Day
and no one can find the President.
Also, there's a milkman
who refuses to deliver.
Oh well, I say, still I've got thirteen
dachshunds, and the woman sleeping on the train
fell off but wasn't hurt
as much as she was just plain surprised.
It's time to go to sleep,
but no one does, everyone's afraid
of falling off.
The World Series was a bust.
And last Christmas
everyone got what they deserved.
I don't mean that sarcastically.
This morning someone threw me a pancake
through their sunroof.
It was just what I needed
when I needed it most.
There's a pet squirrel
watching all of this,

I know that. That pleases me.

Perhaps I'm too easily pleased.

Fritz is the name I gave

to all of my dachshunds.

It seems to please them.

They are benign, all in a pile.

But they refuse to eat, nonetheless.

The guard dog fell to pieces.

Butterflies covered everything,

like a marmalade

that couldn't be staunched.

The heavens opened, the heavens closed.

The weather was inventing a new way

of expressing itself.

This was fine by me, a fine contribution.

There was a tunnel at the end of the fog.

What little meditation I had

was gone in a puff.

It was part of our plans, our city plans,

our even bigger plans, that we should circle

and take shortcuts and maybe even fly over

all those obstacles

that were hitherto our lives.

This was good. We had a big,

unclear sense of this,

and that was exactly what we needed.

Semi-sacred bedtime stories.

Squirt bottles on the windowsill.

We had had enough of picnicking.
One of the court painters
also fell over, and then left
in spectacular disorder.
I opened a resort, a last resort,
and people milled around.
Then the buildings began to arrive
and it was politics as usual
until the woman of my dreams appeared
and it was a day at the races,
not tired, not too sad.
Frank and Lloyd and Betty said
nothing could have improved upon it,
and that was good enough for me.

Head of a White Woman Winking

She has one good bumblebee
which she leads about town
on a leash of clover.
It's as big as a Saint Bernard
but also extremely fragile.
People want to pet its long, shaggy coat.
These would be mostly whirling dervishes
out shopping for accessories.
When Lily winks they understand everything,
right down to the particle
of a butterfly's wing lodged
in her last good eye,
so the situation is avoided,
the potential for a cataclysm
is narrowly averted,
and the bumblebee lugs
its little bundle of shaved nerves
forward, on a mission
from some sick, young godhead.

Like a Scarf

The directions to the lunatic asylum were confusing;
most likely they were the random associations
and confused ramblings of a lunatic.
We arrived three hours late for lunch
and the lunatics were stacked up on their shelves,
quite neatly, I might add, giving credit where credit is due.
The orderlies were clearly very orderly, and they
should receive all the credit that is their due.
When I asked one of the doctors for a corkscrew
he produced one without a moment's hesitation.
And it was a corkscrew of the finest craftsmanship,
very shiny and bright, not unlike the doctor himself.
"We'll be conducting our picnic under the great oak
beginning in just a few minutes, and if you'd care
to join us we'd be most honored. However, I understand
you have your obligations and responsibilities,
and if you would prefer to simply visit with us
from time to time, between patients, our invitation
is nothing if not flexible. And, we shan't be the least slighted
or offended in any way if, due to your heavy load,
we are altogether deprived of the pleasure
of exchanging a few anecdotes, regarding the mentally ill,
depraved, diseased, the purely knavish, you in your bughouse,
if you'll pardon my vernacular, O yes, and we in our crackbrain
daily rounds, there are so many gone potty everywhere we roam,
not to mention in one's own home, dead moonstruck.
Well, well, indeed we would have many notes to compare
if you could find the time to join us after your injections."

My invitation was spoken in the evenest tones,

but midway through it I began to suspect I was addressing

an imposter. I returned the corkscrew in a nonthreatening manner.

What, for instance, I asked myself, would a doctor, a doctor of the mind,

be doing with a corkscrew in his pocket?

This was a very sick man, one might even say dangerous.

I began moving away cautiously, never taking my eyes off of him.

His right eyelid was twitching guiltily, or at least anxiously,

and his smock flapping slightly in the wind.

Several members of our party were mingling with the nurses

down by the duck pond, and my grip on the situation

was loosening, the planks in my picnic platform were rotting.

I was thinking about the potato salad in an unstable environment.

A weeping spell was about to overtake me.

I was very close to howling and gnashing the gladiola.

I noticed the great calm of the clouds overhead.

And below, several nurses appeared to me in need of nursing.

The psychopaths were stirring from their naps,

I should say, their postprandial slumbers.

They were lumbering through the pines like inordinately sad moose.

Who could eat liverwurst at a time like this?

But, then again, what's a picnic without pathos?

Lacking a way home, I adjusted the flap in my head and duckwalked

down to the pond and into the pond and began gliding

around in circles, quacking, quacking like a scarf.

Inside the belly of that image I began

recycling like a sorry whim, sincerest regrets

are always best.

More Later, Less the Same

The common is unusually calm—they captured the storm
last night, it's sleeping in the stockade, relieved
of its duty, pacified, tamed, a pussycat.
But not before it tied the flagpole in knots,
and not before it alarmed the firemen out of their pants.
Now it's really calm, almost too calm, as though
anything could happen, and it would be a first.
It could be the worst thing that ever happened.
All the little rodents are sitting up and counting
their nuts. What if nothing ever happened again?
Would there be enough to "eke out an existence,"
as they say? I wish "they" were here now, kicking
up a little dust, mussing my hair, taunting me
with weird syllogisms. Instead, these are the windless,
halcyon days. The lull dispassion is upon us.
Serenity has triumphed in its mindless, atrophied way.
A school of Stoics walks by, eager, in its phlegmatic way,
to observe human degradation, lust and debauchery
at close quarters. They are disappointed,
but it barely shows on their faces. They are late Stoa,
very late. They missed the bus. They should have
been here last night. The joint was jumping.
But people change, they grow up, they fly around.
It's the same old story, but I don't remember it.
It's a tale of gore and glory, but we had to leave.
It could have turned out differently, and it did.
I feel much the same way about the city of Pompeii.
A police officer with a poodle cut squirts his gun

at me for saying that, and it's still just barely
possible that I didn't, and the clock is running
out on his sort of behavior. I'm napping in a wigwam
as I write this, near Amity Street, which is buried
under fifteen feet of ashes and cinders and rocks.
Moss and a certain herblike creature are beginning to
whisper nearby. I am beside myself, peering down,
senselessly, since, for us, in space, there is
neither above nor below; and thus the expression
"He is being nibbled to death by ducks" shines
with such style, such poise, and reserve,
a beautiful, puissant form and a lucid thought.
To which I reply "It is time we had our teeth examined
by a dentist." So said James the Lesser to James the More.

How the Pope Is Chosen

Any poodle under ten inches high is a toy.

Almost always a toy is an imitation

of something grown-ups use.

Popes with unclipped hair are called *corded popes*.

If a Pope's hair is allowed to grow unchecked,

it becomes extremely long and twists

into long strands that look like ropes.

When it is shorter it is tightly curled.

Popes are very intelligent.

There are three different sizes.

The largest are called standard Popes.

The medium-sized ones are called miniature Popes.

I could go on like this, I could say:

"He is a squarely built Pope, neat,

well-proportioned, with an alert stance

and an expression of bright curiosity,"

but I won't. After a poodle dies

all the cardinals flock to the nearest 7-Eleven.

They drink Slurpees until one of them throws up

and then he's the new Pope.

He is then fully armed and rides through the wilderness alone,

day and night in all kinds of weather.

The new Pope chooses the name he will use as Pope,

like "Wild Bill" or "Buffalo Bill."

He wears red shoes with a cross embroidered on the front.

Most Popes are called "Babe" because

growing up to become a Pope is a lot of fun.

All the time their bodies are becoming bigger and stranger,

but sometimes things happen to make them unhappy.

They have to go to the bathroom by themselves,

and they spend almost all of their time sleeping.

Parents seem to be incapable of helping their little Popes grow up.

Fathers tell them over and over again not to lean out of windows,

but the sky is full of them.

It looks as if they are just taking it easy,

but they are learning something else.

What, we don't know, because we are not like them.

We can't even dress like them.

We are like red bugs or mites compared to them.

We think we are having a good time cutting cartoons out of the paper,

but really we are eating crumbs out of their hands.

We are tiny germs that cannot be seen under microscopes.

When a Pope is ready to come into the world,

we try to sing a song, but the words do not fit the music too well.

Some of the full-bodied Popes are a million times bigger than us.

They open their mouths at regular intervals.

They are continually grinding up pieces of the cross

and spitting them out. Black flies cling to their lips.

Once they are elected they are given a bowl of cream

and a puppy clip. Eyebrows are a protection

when a Pope must plunge through dense underbrush

in search of a sheep.

Becoming a Scout

Alone in my tree house
I can hear snakes thinking—
they want eggs for breakfast,
eggs for lunch and dinner,
all the while under a cloud of frangipani perfume.
This is the snake's dream,
and listening to sitar music.
If I say they are "sloe-eyed,"
I won't know what I mean. Bottle-green,
moiling, with rapier wit,
sending radiograms
to the marcelled, saw-toothed boy named Tony
who is about to major in Natural History somewhere.
I don't know where, exactly.
He opposes progress, though some seems evident,
at least from up here.
I hope you don't think I am being namby-pamby
when I say frog spittle is upon me.
I belong to several City Garden Clubs
and I know what I mean.
I know the right way and the wrong way
of bracing a crotch in a tree.
Also, a hundred pounds of tree food
is worth more than a hundred hours of cavity work.
There are a lot of frauds in the tree surgery racket.
Well, I digress. What got me off?
Tony, the maladjusted Naturalist.
There are several things necessary

to understanding the snake mentality:

they have air pumps in the oral cavity region.

That's all. Well, I could add

that the thermoscopic eyes of the squid

perceive the heat-generating object

through photochemical reactions,

which is completely different—I mean,

this is so unsnakelike as to be irrelevant.

Let's pretend I never mentioned this last bit.

My mind is drifting, as if on a leaf, on a wave,

a warm current is pulling my brains out, away, away from me.

Therefore I must proceed in a thoughtless, indeed brainless,

fashion, which could prove painful,

though I shall barely notice.

My best friend is a black squirrel

and he is too busy to visit me just now.

His name is Fester N. Wildly.

I don't know what the N stands for.

Perhaps Norman. Or Nothing.

He has been married for five years

and is an automotive parts salesman.

What else do I know about Fester, my dear, dear friend?

Oh yes, he has fourteen children,

three of whom still live at home.

His wife's name is Arlene

and she is originally from Cincinnati.

In the evenings they like to play bridge.

They have a statue of me on their mantel.

They have me over to dinner on a regular basis,

like once a year, maybe. She calls me Perkwu,

though that is not even close to my real name.

My name is Spoimo, which I find strange.

Annual Report

Only one Disorderly Person was reported.

(No one cared enough to report me.)

Likewise, only one Noise Complaint.

(Can the whole village be deaf?)

And, in an entire year, there was only one

case of Indecent Exposure.

(Is no one paying attention?)

Talk about breaking records, in all of 1989

there was only one Disturbed Person.

(I hope they spelled my name right.)

On the bright side, eleven persons

were reported missing, and thirty-six

were identified as Suspicious.

Three motor vehicles were abandoned.

And there were five Deer Complaints.

(Well pardon us for existing.)

An Eland, in Retirement

Once the eland was very common,
and traveled in large herds
over the plains of Africa.
But the eland was not a very fast runner,
and it could not defend itself
or get away from its enemies.
Now there is only one, and it lives
in Teaneck, New Jersey—pop. 37,825—
and watches television from
early morning until late at night.
It likes Pop-Tarts and little else.
Memories of Africa: it was shaped
like a pear, a few men in turbans
and long flowing robes, wandering
giants with very fancy hairstyles
beating drums, and women with
dinner plates in their lips.
Did you know that Mamie Eisenhower's
engagement ring was an exact duplicate
of Dwight's West Point ring, specially
made to fit her hand? Tidbits
such as that have made all of
my aggravation endurable. They were married
on July 1, 1916, in Denver, Colorado.
Mamie's full maiden name was Mary
Geneva Doud and she was born in Boone, Iowa,
on November 14, 1896. Is Mamie still alive?
It seems as if she is. She seldom hunted, I'm told.

Mami, Mami, Mami, we hardly knew ya.
The less said about "Bess" Truman—
née Elizabeth Virginia Wallace—the better.
I'd rather talk about the salubrious effects
of a bite by a tsetse fly, or the kindness
of cheetahs. Harry called her "the Boss,"
but Harry loved all of his women,
even Margaret. Like an earthworm,
she had a soft body, and like an earthworm
she had no eyes or ears or arms or legs.
I'm just saying that because I am the last
eland and nobody cares, at least nobody in Teaneck.
Margaret Truman was born in 1924.
She played the tuba (I'm joking) and was not very good.
Since moving to America, I have become
very interested in sculpture, and I am particularly
fond of the works of Augustus Saint-Gaudens.
He died in 1907, and his estate in Cornish, N.H.,
has been made a memorial to him, with plaster
and bronze replicas of his work.
His memorial to Clover Adams, Henry Adams'
strange and difficult wife, has puzzled generations.
Clover's suicide and Henry's benign acceptance
is still a cloud to behold in wonder.
Which reminds me: egg noodles of the best grade,
made of fresh eggs and selected wheat flour,
are highly nutritious and are easily digested
even by delicate stomachs, and they are frequently

recommended for invalids and convalescents.

Lobsters afford more phosphorus than any other food.

They are, perhaps unconsciously, on this account

much eaten by the nerve-racked workers of the great cities.

As you can see, I have taken it upon myself

to keep abreast of the times, as unlikely as it is

that I will have an opportunity to pass on this information

to any successor. I have, for the record, agreed

to three "dates" since the last of my kind passed on:

the first was with an impala; it had a very attractive

purple-black blaze on its forehead, and moved

with great grace, but finally it was too jumpy.

It would jump ten feet over nothing, and this seemed to me

entirely unnecessary and unnerving. The second

was a disaster: a wildebeest by the name of Norman.

Norman would run around in circles snorting,

tossing his head as if it were on fire.

This was not my idea of a good time.

My last attempt at finding a mate is better left untold.

A bat-eared fox. I was desperate, and temporarily

lost all sense of decorum, for which I am truly chagrined.

He was cute, a fine pet, perhaps, but hardly

a suitable father for my progeny.

A red sleeve, that's all I know, a red sleeve

reaches through me. I can dress wounds,

endure night duty, but I have never been

to the cinema. In fact, by now I am old and cranky

and it's all that I can do to change the channel

and watch these little people solve their crimes,

so dear to their hearts. They are all selling

sanitation products on the side, or mainly.

Why was I spared, I'll never know.

In the vast savanna scrub

a melancholy bug preens its antennae

in the glow of the worn-out sun.

Bureaucratic gossip, don't take any notice of it.

The New Work

The great cat was dreaming of me,

but each time it tried

it fell just short of imagining the vastness of my nights.

So it said, let's start with a little thing,

like his socks, and then, with some luck, we'll build from there.

His socks, with great celestial storms woven around them,

are slipping as he strides across

the ancient war-torn cities whistling an unknown anthem.

(This is very promising: I can see he is a noble figure

out of his mind with grief—the very stuff of poetry!)

When a small dog dashes from an alley and nips at his ankles

he appears dazed and confused—who'd have thought

he was so fragile, all that wisdom and courage

so easily dispersed. He peers around through the crowd

as if searching for some familiar reference point.

The dog licks his hands and he appears sheepishly grateful.

The whole scene has passed unremarked upon by the passersby,

who, in contrast now, seem to be charged with splendid missions:

the maid with her baguette hoists her banner straight into the slaughter;

the unshaven worker in his grimy overalls rescues her from oblivion

by doffing his cap and bowing slightly.

An officer from a nearby bank is stirring a single cube of sugar

into his demitasse: he knows that worker,

and takes a modicum of satisfaction in recalling

the loan he refused to grant him the Christmas before last.

But that is neither here nor there. The sun is breaking through the clouds

for the first time in more than a week.

The great cat has turned its eye elsewhere,

and while at first I was flattered to think that my poor self

could be elevated by such attention I readily confess to the doubt

the whole project filled me with, though doubt itself does seem deserving

of an immense meditation, ending, no doubt, with all those fine details

we can't seem to escape—the perfume clinging to a paper clip,

the hedge clippers in the bathtub.

The great cat is pacing the floor

(I can't see him but I sense him everywhere).

He wants to start over, he wants most of all to edit me out.

His new work begins: "The simoom is a strong, dry wind

that spreads mayonnaise over the deserts of North Africa."

Inspiration

The two men sat roasting in their blue suits

on the edge of a mustard field.

Lucien Cardin, a local painter,

had suggested a portrait.

President and Vice President of the bank branch,

maybe it would hang in the lobby

inspiring confidence. It might even

cast a little grace and dignity

on the citizens of their hamlet.

They were serious men with sober thoughts

about an unstable world.

The elder, Gilbert, smoked his pipe

and gazed through his wire-rims beyond the painter.

The sky was eggshell blue,

and Lucien knew what he was doing

when he begged their pardon

and went to fetch the two straw hats.

They were farmers' hats, for working in the sun.

Gilbert and Tom agreed to wear them

to staunch their perspiration,

but they knew too the incongruity

their appearance now suggested.

And, as for the lobby of their bank,

solidarity with the farmers, their customers.

The world might go to war—Louis flattened

Schmeling the night before—but a portrait
was painted that day in a field of mustard
outside of Alexandria, Ontario,
of two men, even-tempered and levelheaded,
and of what they did next there is no record.

Worshipful Company of Fletchers

I visited the little boy
at the edge of the woods.
It's still not clear to me
where he really lives.
He'd live with animals
if they'd take him in,
and there would never be
a need to speak. "Who knows,
when you grow up you may be
President," I said, trying
to break the spell.
He flinched as though struck.
"Perhaps something in the field
of numismatics," I continued,
"would be less stressful.
A correspondence school course.
No need to leave the home,
no wretched professor thwacking
your knuckles. In no time
you could hang out your shingle—
STAMPS AND COINS. No more than
one customer per week,
I feel fairly certain: some nerd
who can barely talk—
I'm certainly not speaking of
yourself here—browsing
the Liberty dimes and Indian head
pennies, if you see what I mean."

I had meant to comfort him,
but the feral child was now
mewling, and this annoyed me.
"I doubt you have what it takes—
discipline, fastidiousness,
honesty, devotion—to serve
as a manservant, a butler,
to a gentleman of rank and
high-calling. No, I'm afraid
no amount of training
could instill those virtues
into one such as you."
I paused to let the acid burn.
The doe-eyed lad wiped his nose
on his tee-shirt and peeked over
his shoulder into the woods
which seemed to beckon him.
A breeze rustled the leaves
above our heads, and the boy swayed.
A pileated woodpecker tapped
some Morse code into a dead oak tree.
At last, the boy said, "You regret
everything, I bet. You came here
with a crude notion of righting
all that was wrong with your own
bitter childhood, but you have become
your own father—cruel, taunting—
who had become his father, and so on.

It's such a common story.
I wish I could say to you:
'You'd make a fine shepherd,'
but you wouldn't. Your tireless needs
would consume you the first night."
And, with that, the boy stepped forward
and kissed me on the cheek.

Happy As the Day Is Long

I take the long walk up the staircase to my secret room.

Today's big news: they found Amelia Earhart's shoe, size 9.

1992: Charlie Christian is bebopping at Minton's in 1941.

Today, the Presidential primaries have failed us once again.

We'll look for our excitement elsewhere, in the last snow

that is falling, in tomorrow's Gospel Concert in Springfield.

It's a good day to be a cat and just sleep.

Or to read the *Confessions* of Saint Augustine.

Jesus called the sons of Zebedee the Sons of Thunder.

In my secret room, plans are hatched: we'll explore the Smoky Mountains.

Then we'll walk along a beach: Hallelujah!

(A letter was just delivered by Overnight Express—

it contained nothing of importance, I slept through it.)

(I guess I'm trying to be "above the fray.")

The Russians, I know, have developed a language called *Lincos*

designed for communicating with the inhabitants of other worlds.

That's been a waste of time, not even a postcard.

But then again, there are tree-climbing fish, called anabases.

They climb the trees out of stupidity, or so it is said.

Who am I to judge? I want to break out of here.

A bee is not strong in geometry: it cannot tell

a square from a triangle or a circle.

The locker room of my skull is full of panting egrets.

I'm saying that strictly for effect.

In time I will heal, I know this, or I believe this.

The contents and furnishings of my secret room will be labeled

and organized so thoroughly it will be a little frightening.

What I thought was infinite will turn out to be just a couple
of odds and ends, a tiny miscellany, miniature stuff, fragments
of novelties, of no great moment. But it will also be enough,
maybe even more than enough, to suggest an immense ritual and tradition.
And this makes me very happy.

SHROUD OF
THE GNOME

Where Babies Come From

Many are from the Maldives,
southwest of India, and must begin
collecting shells almost immediately.
The larger ones may prefer coconuts.
Survivors move from island to island
hopping over one another and never
looking back. After the typhoons
have had their pick, and the birds of prey
have finished with theirs, the remaining few
must build boats, and in this, of course,
they can have no experience, they build
their boats of palm leaves and vines.
Once the work is completed, they lie down,
thoroughly exhausted and confused,
and a huge wave washes them out to sea.
And that is the last they see of one another.
In their dreams Mama and Papa
are standing on the shore
for what seems like an eternity,
and it is almost always the wrong shore.

Days of Pie and Coffee

A motorist once said to me,
and this was in the country,
on a county lane, a motorist
slowed his vehicle as I was
walking my dear old collie,
Sithney, by the side of the road,
and the motorist came to a halt
mildly alarming both Sithney and myself,
not yet accustomed to automobiles,
and this particular motorist
sent a little spasm of fright up our spines,
which in turn panicked the driver a bit
and it seemed as if we were off to a bad start,
and that's when Sithney began to bark
and the man could not be heard, that is,
if he was speaking or trying to speak
because I was commanding Sithney to be silent,
though, indeed I was sympathetic
to his emotional excitement.
It was, as I recall, a day of prodigious beauty.
April 21, 1932—clouds,
like the inside of your head explained.
Bluebirds, too numerous to mention.
The clover calling you by name.
And fields oozing green.
And this motorist from nowhere
moving his lips
like the wings of a butterfly
and nothing coming out,

and Sithney silent now.

He was no longer looking at us,

but straight ahead

where his election was in doubt.

"That's a fine dog," he said.

"Collies are made in heaven."

"Well, if I were a voting man I'd vote for you," I said.

"A bedoozling day to be lost in the country, I say.

Leastways, I am a misplaced individual."

We introduced ourselves

and swapped a few stories.

He was a veteran and a salesman

who didn't believe in his product—

I've forgotten what it was—hair restorer,

parrot feed—and he enjoyed nothing more

than a day spent meandering the back roads

in his jalopy. I gave him directions

to the Denton farm, but I doubt

that he followed them, he didn't

seem to be listening, and it was getting late

and Sithney had an idea of his own

and I don't know why I am remembering this now,

just that he summed himself up by saying

"I've missed too many boats"

and all these years later

I keep thinking that was a man

who loved to miss boats,

but he didn't miss them that much.

A Knock on the Door

They ask me if I've ever thought
about the end of the world,
and I say, "Come in, come in,
let me give you some lunch, for God's sake."
After a few bites it's the afterlife
they want to talk about. "Ouch," I say,
"did you see that grape leaf skeletonizer?"
Then they're talking about redemption
and the chosen few sitting right by His side.
"Doing what?" I ask. "Just sitting?"
I am surrounded by burned up zombies.
"Let's have some lemon chiffon pie
I bought yesterday at the 3 Dog Bakery."
But they want to talk about my soul.
I'm getting drowsy and see butterflies
everywhere. "Would you gentlemen
like to take a nap, I know I would."
They stand and back away from me,
out the door, walking toward my neighbors,
a black cloud over their heads
and they see nothing without end.

Never Again the Same

Speaking of sunsets,

last night's was shocking.

I mean, sunsets aren't supposed to frighten you, are they?

Well, this one was terrifying.

People were screaming in the streets.

Sure, it was beautiful, but far too beautiful.

It wasn't natural.

One climax followed another and then another

until your knees went weak

and you couldn't breathe.

The colors were definitely not of this world,

peaches dripping opium,

pandemonium of tangerines,

inferno of irises,

Plutonian emeralds,

all swirling and churning, swabbing,

like it was playing with us,

like we were nothing,

as if our whole lives were a preparation for this,

this for which nothing could have prepared us

and for which we could not have been less prepared.

The mockery of it all stung us bitterly.

And when it was finally over

we whimpered and cried and howled.

And then the streetlights came on as always

and we looked into one another's eyes—

ancient caves with still pools

and those little transparent fish

who have never seen even one ray of light.

And the calm that returned to us

was not even our own.

Restless Leg Syndrome

After the burial
we returned to our units
and assumed our poses.
Our posture was the new posture
and not the old sick posture.
When we left our stations
it was just to prove we could,
not a serious departure
or a search for yet another beginning.
We were done with all that.
We were settled in, as they say,
thought it might have been otherwise.
What a story!
After the burial we returned to our units
and here is where I am experiencing
that leg-kicking syndrome thing.
My leg, for no apparent reason,
flies around the room kicking stuff,
well, whatever is in its way,
like a screen or a watering can.
Those are just two examples
and indeed I could give many more.
I could construct a catalogue
of the things it kicks,
perhaps I will do that later.
We'll just have to see if it's really wanted.
Or I could do a little now
and then return to listing later.

It kicked the scrimshaw collection,
yes it did. It kicked the ocelot,
which was rude and uncalled for,
and yes hurtful. It kicked
the guacamole right out of its bowl,
which made for a grubby
and potentially dangerous workplace.
I was out testing the new speed bump
when it kicked the viscountess,
which she probably deserved,
and I was happy, needless to say,
to not be a witness.
The kicking subsided for a while,
nobody was keeping track of time
at that time so it is impossible
to fill out the forms accurately.
Suffice it to say we remained
at our units on constant alert.
And then it kicked over the little cow town
we had set up for punching and that sort of thing,
a covered wagon filled with cover girls.
But now it was kicked over
and we had a moment of silence,
but it was clear to me
that many of our minions
were getting tetchy
and some of them were getting tetchier.
And then it kicked a particularly treasured snuff box

which, legend has it, once belonged to somebody
named Bob Mackey, so we were understandably
saddened and returned to our units rather weary.
No one seemed to think I was in the least bit culpable.
It was my leg, of course, that was doing the actual kicking,
of that I am almost certain.
At any rate, we decided to bury it.
After the burial we returned to our units
and assumed our poses.
A little bit of time passed, not much,
and then John's leg started acting suspicious.
It looked like it wanted to kick the replica
of the White House we keep on hand
just for situations such as this.
And then, sure enough, it did.

The Blind Heron

Now Kiki's gone and lost her cockatiel, Lilith.

She's put signs up all over town offering a reward.

I don't hold out much hope for Lilith's return.

Given our New England climate she's probably

halfway to Australia by now. Kiki mopes around

feeling rejected, of course, taking it personally,

of course, as if Lilith were the final judge.

And it is true, Kiki has her problems: she's a liar,

for one thing, and not just your average prevaricator.

Kiki once arrived at a party at my house and announced

to everyone that "the President has just been shot."

We turned on the radio immediately, and it was true

the President had just been shot, but Kiki didn't

know this, it was her idea of an entrance,

or so we thought. But perhaps that was a poor example

of Kiki's essentially prevaricating nature.

Okay. One time I asked Kiki what she did over the weekend.

She said: "I went to Tasmania." That's nice, I said,

but please don't insult my credulity. Tasmania, hmmm.

What's the capital of Tasmania? "Hobart," she said.

"I captured a very nice cockatiel while I was there.

Would you care to meet it?" Well, I met Lilith,

a nice-looking bird, very nice, but I really don't think

Lilith is her real name. If I had flown to Tasmania

for the weekend and had captured a fine bird like that

I would have called her Christina the Astonishing,

I would have known beyond a doubt that that was her true name.

Why Kiki lies about such elementary truths is beyond me.
You can see why I considered it my duty to remove the bird
from Kiki's care, poor Kiki, and beautiful, glorious
Christina the Astonishing, who, by the way, is from
Australia, not Tasmania, of that I am almost certain.

Acting on a Tip

We went to the bug-eating state.
We sat down on some little bluestem grass.
Grasshoppers plague the state.
So who's eating the bugs?
Acting on a tip, we brushed our teeth.
This was going to be a very long drive.
Recumbent bison decorated the airwaves.
Acting on a tip, I got dressed and walked
down to the river and washed my face
and combed my hair and picked the bugs
from my teeth and urinated on a leaf.
The leaf was a moving target
as a crack squadron of soldier ants
had big plans for it elsewhere.
My yellow rain was meant to amuse them,
nothing more. What a glorious morning
for bugs in general, for caterpillars
speeding toward their destiny in the sky,
dragonflies mating in flight,
ancient beetles lugging their excess wisdom
to the auction block, and katydids
in charge of cryptography, and walking sticks
to remind us of how long the road can be.
And this is by no means an exhaustive catalogue.
One could prattle on about a variety of mites
until the cows come home. Instead,
let's talk about cows no more.
Acting on a tip, I zipped up

and returned to the beefsteak club in progress,
the raving, looting, windswept, boomeranging
family of vacationers to which I belong.
They were seated on a log discussing pork futures.
My beloved daughter Tabitha was breathing heavily.
There was a common earwig exiting her right ear,
or so I told her. "Daddy," she replied,
"that earwigs crawl into people's ears at night
and bite them is a totally unfounded superstition.
Earwigs are harmless, only occasionally damaging
flower blossoms." I scanned the horizon.
"Let's camp here," I said. "But Daddy,"
they announced in unison, "we *are* camped here."

Shroud of the Gnome

And what amazes me is that none of our modern inventions
surprise or interest him, even a little. I tell him
it is time he got his booster shots, but then
I realize I have no power over him whatsoever.
He becomes increasingly light-footed until I lose sight
of him downtown between the federal building and
the post office. A registered nurse is taking her
coffee break. I myself needed a break, so I sat down
next to her at the counter. "Don't mind me," I said,
"I'm just a hungry little Gnostic in need of a sandwich."
(This old line of mine had met with great success
on any number of previous occasions.) I thought,
a deaf, dumb, and blind nurse, sounds ideal!
But then I remembered that some of the earliest
Paleolithic office workers also feigned blindness
when approached by nonoffice workers, so I paid my bill
and disappeared down an alley where I composed myself.
Amid the piles of outcast citizenry and burning barrels
of waste and rot, the plump rats darting freely,
the havoc of blown newspapers, lay the little shroud
of my lost friend: small and grey and threadbare,
windworn by the ages of scurrying hither and thither,
battered by the avalanches and private tornadoes
of just being a gnome, but surely there were good times, too.
And now, rejuvenated by the wind, the shroud moves forward,
hesitates, dances sideways, brushes my foot as if for a kiss,
and flies upward, whistling a little-known ballad
about the pitiful, raw etiquette of the underworld.

My Felisberto

My felisberto is handsomer than your mergotroid,

although, admittedly, your mergotroid may be the wiser of the two.

Whereas your mergotroid never winces or quails,

my felisberto is a titan of inconsistencies.

For a night of wit and danger and temptation

my felisberto would be the obvious choice.

However, at dawn or dusk when serenity is desired

your mergotroid cannot be ignored.

Merely to sit near it in the garden

and watch the fabrications of the world swirl by,

the deep-sea's bathymetry wash your eyes,

not to mention the little fawns of the forest

and their flip-floppy gymnastics, ah, for this

and so much more your mergotroid is infinitely preferable.

But there is a place for darkness and obscurity

without which life can sometimes seem too much,

too frivolous and too profound simultaneously,

and that is when my felisberto is needed,

is longed for and loved, and then the sun can rise again.

The bee and the hummingbird drink of the world,

and your mergotroid elaborates the silent concert

that is always and always about to begin.

Same as You

I put my pants on one day at a time.
Then I hop around in circles hobbledehoy.
A projectile of some sort pokes me
in the eye—I think it's a bird
or a flying pyramid that resembles a bird.
Well it sure hurts and I'm swelling
even in areas where it's inappropriate
such as my cupola, also my cup of tea.
Flapdoodle is my middle name so I know
two specks about what's coming next:
the leopard's spots and their humorous sayings.
There are those who would suggest that
I am hog-tied and frequently late to work.
To which I reply: Indeed I am.
As a former ranchero and postmodern
farmerette I think we can speak freely
of the current crisis—the soil is creeping
out from under us and the haycocks
appear lubberly. If it's true
that you can judge a man's character
by the shape of his sandcastle,
then I say you are a squint-eyed stormy petrel,
and I a piebald crabstick,
which is like a dream come true.
We're practically carved out of the same carrot.
I for one can barely tell where I trail off
and you begin, since human beings are reported
to be ninety-eight percent duct tape

and feathers anyway. It's hard
to pull the pants on over all of this debris,
and once the greensward has been wrenched
into shape the going is so smooth
it's almost like not going at all.
Where have I been, where have I been?
Thus I was led into paths I had not known.

Shut Up and Eat Your Toad

The disorganization to which I currently belong
has skipped several meetings in a row
which is a pattern I find almost fatally attractive.
Down at headquarters there's a secretary
and a janitor who I shall call Suzie
and boy can she ever shoot straight.
She'll shoot you straight in the eye if you ask her to.
I mow the grass every other Saturday
and that's the day she polishes the trivets
whether they need it or not, I don't know
if there is a name for this kind of behavior,
hers or mine, but somebody once said something or another.
That's why I joined up in the first place,
so somebody could teach me a few useful phrases,
such as, "Good afternoon, my dear anal-retentive Doctor,"
and "My, that is a lovely dictionary you have on, Mrs. Smith."
Still, I hardly feel like functioning even on a brute
or loutish level. My plants think I'm one of them,
and they don't look so good themselves, or so
I tell them. I like to give them at least several
reasons to be annoyed with me, it's how they exercise
their skinny spectrum of emotions. Because.
That and cribbage. Often when I return from the club
late at night, weary-laden, weary-winged, washed out,
I can actually hear the nematodes working, sucking
the juices from the living cells of my narcissus.
I have mentioned this to Suzie on several occasions.
Each time she has backed away from me, panic-stricken,

when really I was just making a stab at conversation.

It is not my intention to alarm anyone, but dear Lord

if I find a dead man in the road and his eyes

are crawling with maggots, I refuse to say

have a nice day Suzie just because she's desperate

and her life is a runaway carriage rushing toward a cliff

now can I? Would you let her get away with that kind of crap?

Who are you anyway? And what kind of disorganization is this?

Baron of the Holy Grail? Well it's about time you got here.

I was worried, I was starting to fret.

Lafcadio

He was never mean to me.

I never once heard him speak ill of another.

And he was always good by his word.

If he said he was bringing over a brace of quail

you set the table then and there.

Best of all, he was punctual,

a virtue I dearly love in a dog.

And he never crept, never crept, never crept.

Nonstop

It seemed as if the enormous journey
was finally approaching its conclusion.
From the window of the train
the last trees were dissipating,
a childlike sailor waved once,
a seal-like dog barked and died.
The conductor entered the lavatory
and was not seen again, although
his harmonica-playing was appreciated.
He was not without talent, some said.
A botanist with whom I had become acquainted
actually suggested we form a group or something.
I was looking for a familiar signpost
in his face, or a landmark that would
indicate the true colors of his tribe.
But, alas, there was not a glass of water
anywhere or even the remains of a trail.
I got a bewildered expression of my own
and slinked to the back of the car
where a nun started to tickle me.
She confided to me that it was her
cowboy pride that got her through. . . .
Through what? I thought, but drew my hand
close to an imaginary vest.
"That's a beautiful vest," she said,
as I began crawling down the aisle.
At last, I pressed my face against
the window: A little frog was licking

its chop, as was the stationmaster

licking something. We didn't stop.

We didn't appear to be arriving,

and yet we were almost out of landscape.

No creeks or rivers. Nothing

even remotely reminding one of a mound.

O mound! thou ain't around no more.

A heap of abstract geometrical symbols,

that's what it's coming to, I thought.

A nothing you could sink your teeth into.

"Relief's on the way," a little

know-nothing boy said to me.

"Imagine my surprise," I said

and reached out to muss his hair.

But he had no hair and it felt unlucky

touching his skull like that.

"Forget what I said," he said.

"What did you say?" I asked

in automatic compliance.

And then it got very dark and quiet.

I closed my eyes and dreamed of an emu I once loved.

Dream On

Some people go their whole lives
without ever writing a single poem.
Extraordinary people who don't hesitate
to cut somebody's heart or skull open.
They go to baseball games with the greatest of ease
and play a few rounds of golf as if it were nothing.
These same people stroll into a church
as if that were a natural part of life.
Investing money is second nature to them.
They contribute to political campaigns
that have absolutely no poetry in them
and promise none for the future.
They sit around the dinner table at night
and pretend as though nothing is missing.
Their children get caught shoplifting at the mall
and no one admits that it is poetry they are missing.
The family dog howls all night,
lonely and starving for more poetry in his life.
Why is it so difficult for them to see
that, without poetry, their lives are effluvial.
Sure, they have their banquets, their celebrations,
croquet, fox hunts, their seashores and sunsets,
their cocktails on the balcony, dog races,
and all that kissing and hugging, and don't
forget the good deeds, the charity work,
nursing the baby squirrels all through the night,
filling the birdfeeders all winter,
helping the stranger change her tire.

Still, there's that disagreeable exhalation

from decaying matter, subtle but ever present.

They walk around erect like champions.

They are smooth-spoken, urbane and witty.

When alone, rare occasion, they stare

into the mirror for hours, bewildered.

There was something they meant to say, but didn't:

"And if we put the statue of the rhinoceros

next to the tweezers, and walk around the room three times,

learn to yodel, shave our heads, call

our ancestors back from the dead—"

poetrywise it's still a bust, bankrupt.

You haven't scribbled a syllable of it.

You're a nowhere man misfiring

the very essence of your life, flustering

nothing from nothing and back again.

The hereafter may not last all that long.

Radiant childhood sweetheart,

secret code of everlasting joy and sorrow,

fanciful pen strokes beneath the eyelids:

all day, all night meditation, knot of hope,

kernel of desire, pure ordinariness of life,

seeking, through poetry, a benediction

or a bed to lie down on, to connect, reveal,

explore, to imbue meaning on the day's extravagant labor.

And yet it's cruel to expect too much.

It's a rare species of bird

that refuses to be categorized.

Its song is barely audible.
It is like a dragonfly in a dream—
here, then there, then here again,
low-flying amber-wing darting upward
and then out of sight.
And the dream has a pain in its heart
the wonders of which are manifold,
or so the story is told.

Chronology of Events

God knows we've never thought of you
as insufficiently frou-frou.
I actually said that this morning
to my coffee, and the word *recherché*
was not far away, scowling at me.
I had a stranglehold on a straw man,
the son of a bitch was dying fast,
and then I let go and floated for a while.
Time passed like a butterfly in the room.
Suddenly I was in a bathtub, sinking.
And then I was on a couch for a long,
long time, and the butterfly landed
on me and held me in its scissors grip.
Page upon page of blank transcript.
A room inched sideways only slightly.
A nuthatch clung to the windowscreen.
Moments of great clarity inhabited me,
I was their anthill and they were my ants.
And they too must sleep, according to
a lot of prophets. And they will be
nameless, yes, and faceless, yes.
The prophets will boss them around
and insult their mothers, and the little ants
of clarity will just work harder and harder,
for they are blind and dedicated
and stupid, stupid, stupid.
This was revealed to me around 2:24 P.M., 9/27/95.

I Left My Couch in Tatamagouche

I desired lemonade—

It was hot and I had been walking for hours—

but after much wrestling,

pushing and shoving,

I simply could not get my couch

through the restaurant door.

Several customers and the owner

and the owner's son

were kinder than they should have been,

but finally it was time to close

and I urged them to return to their homes,

their families needed them

(the question of who needs what

was hardly my field of expertise).

That night, while sleeping peacefully

outside the train station

on my little, green couch,

I met a giantess by the name of Anna Swan.

She knelt beside my couch

and stroked my brow with tenderness.

She was like a mother to me

for a few moments there under the night sky.

In the morning, I left my couch in Tatamagouche,

and that has made a big difference.

The New Ergonomics

The new ergonomics were delivered
just before lunchtime
so we ignored them.
Without revealing the particulars
let me just say that
lunch was most satisfying.
Jack and Roberta went with
the corned beef for a change.
Jack believes in alien abduction
and Roberta does not,
although she has had
several lost weekends lately
and one or two unexplained scars
on her buttocks. I thought
I recognized someone
from my childhood
at a table across the room,
the same teeth, the same hair,
but when he stood up,
I wasn't sure, Squid with a red tie?
Impossible. I finished
my quiche lorraine
and returned my thoughts
to Jack's new jag:
"Well, I guess anything's
possible. People disappear
all the time, and most of them
have no explanation

when and if they return.
Look at Tony's daughter
and she's never been the same."
Jack was looking as if
he'd bet on the right horse now.
"And these new ergonomics,
who really designed them?
Does anybody know?
Do they tell us anything?
A name, an address? Hell no."
Squid was paying his bill
in a standard-issue blue blazer.
He looked across the room at me
several times. He looked tired,
like he wanted to sleep for a long time
in a barn somewhere, in Kansas.
I wanted to sleep there, too.

MEMOIR OF
THE HAWK

Vale of the White Horse

That's where I first met my bride. She
was standing under a chestnut tree during a
summer shower. I stopped my car and offered
to give her a lift. She didn't seem to hear me.
I got out of the car and walked up to her.
Her skin looked and felt like porcelain. "Are
you okay?" I asked. She blinked her eyes as if
coming out of trance. "I was looking for
the white horse," she said. I drove her to
a hospital where the doctor diagnosed her as
being my bride. "There's no doubt about it,
she is your bride." We kissed, and thus the Trans-
Canadian Highway was born.

Young Man with a Ham

I'm watching him from my window. He's clutching
the ham as if it were a football everyone wants
to steal. He keeps looking over his shoulder and
stopping to make sure the ham is secure in his grip.
No one's on the street but him. But wait, old Mr. Wilson,
who lives down the street from me, has suddenly
appeared in his fedora and suspenders and is jogging
as best he can after the young man. I go out onto
the porch to watch. The young man has not yet seen
Mr. Wilson. Then in the last minute he spots him
and starts to run. To my great amazement, Mr. Wilson
dives through the air and tackles him. They wrestle
and grunt. Mr. Wilson wrenches the ham free, gets
away and starts racing down the street with the ham.
Clearly it's his ham now.

The Lovely Arc of a Meteor in the Night Sky

At the party there were those sage souls
who swam along the bottom like those huge white
fish who live for hundreds of years but have no
fun. They are nearly blind and need the cold.
William was a stingray guarding his cave. Only
those prepared for mortal battle came close to
him. Closer to the surface the smaller fish
played, swimming in mixed patterns only a god
could decipher. They gossiped and fed and sparred
and consumed, and some no doubt even spawned.
It's a life filled with agitation, thrills,
melodrama and twittery, but too soon it's over.
And nothing's revealed because it was never known.

Cunning

I had gotten a nasty bite at the petting
zoo earlier that day. On the bus home I sat
next to a little old lady, tiny and stooped,
her head bobbing up and down. I don't know why
I did this, but I showed her the bite on my hand.
She stared at it for a long time. Then she
reached out and took my hand in her papery
blue-veined hands. She brought my hand closer
to her eyes. Her mouth was open just a little
and my heart started to race. I jerked my
hand out of her grip just in time. She smiled
and showed me her teeth. "They're beautiful,"
I said. "Brand new," she replied.

Overheard on the Driving Range

"Did you ever meet Old Anthony Now-Now?"

"Yes, I'm proud to say I did have the good fortune
to meet Old Anthony Now-Now. Even in his dotage he could
sew a button on a jet plane."

"And he was a wonderful kisser. One night at a party
he asked me what was the most times I had ever been kissed.
I told him the Father of French Surgery had once kissed me
two hundred and seventy-six times in an evening, and Old
Anthony, after asking my approval, proceeded to kiss me
two hundred and seventy-five times, stopping, he said,
so as not to be disrespectful. Fine kisses they were, too."

"The Little Man of Twickenham kissed me for seven hours
straight once and we barely took a breath in all that time.
They were once in a lifetime kisses I'll never forget."

"Did I mention The Discrowned Glutton?"

"Not today."

"Now, there was a poor kisser."

"I think we'd both agree that nobody can compare with
The Illustrious Conqueror of Common Sense. He only kissed
me once but it was as if a bird of paradise shot through
my whole body and I woke more alive than I've ever been."

"Oh, yes, even better than The Bee-Lipped Oracle!"

Endless Time

The donkey stood alone in the paddock
swishing its tail to rid itself of flies.
It was a hot day, but billowing white clouds
occasionally blocked out the sun's rays.
The donkey shook its head and wiggled its
ears, blinked its eyes and now and then
kicked its legs. At night, when no one is
around, it leaps over the barns and turns
somersaults in the air. It is a way of
relieving tension, the donkey's mother
explains to the farmer's wife.

Slow Day at Manny's

Appliances were on our minds all morning.
We tried changing subjects: "That holy war
is a real doozy, isn't she?" Or:
"How's your mother doing? I'm sorry I asked."
Nothing worked. Every attempt ended biliously.
So I finally suggested that we go on down
to Manny's, not to buy anything, but just
to hang out for a while, mingle with the merchandise.
And it felt good, it was a relief to touch
the newfangled, glass-topped stoves, the automatic
ice-making refrigerators, the huge wide-screened
TVs. The two salesmen tried out some small talk
with us, and we politely asked a few relevant
questions. I started watching a game show playing
on about fifteen televisions simultaneously.
I thought, so this must be how a fly sees,
and I was feeling very fly-like and I liked it.
I didn't want to stop being a fly, I was just
pausing in my fly-life to watch this human
game show because I apparently had nothing
more pressing to do just then and I wanted
to know how they lived and what they lived for.
I was glad I was a fly until Josie tapped me
on my head and I looked around and she had
a blender under her arm and I flew around the room

several times buzzing my little brains out.
It was a slow day at Manny's until we got there.
One of the salesmen was named Doctor Ecstaticus
and he was a famous mystic who just happened
to believe in the healing power of appliances.

The Workforce

Do you have adequate oxen for the job?

No, my oxen are inadequate.

Well, how many oxen would it take to do an adequate job?

I would need ten more oxen to do the job adequately.

I'll see if I can get them for you.

I'd be obliged if you could do that for me.

Certainly. And do you have sufficient fishcakes for the men?

We have fifty fishcakes, which is less than sufficient.

I'll have them delivered on the morrow.

Do you need maps of the mountains and the underworld?

We have maps of the mountains but we lack maps of the underworld.

Of course you lack maps of the underworld,

there are no maps of the underworld.

And, besides, you don't want to go there, it's stuffy.

I had no intention of going there, or anywhere for that matter.

It's just that you asked me if I needed maps. . . .

Yes, yes, it's my fault, I got carried away.

What do you need, then, you tell me?

We need seeds, we need plows, we need scythes, chickens,

pigs, cows, buckets and women.

Women?

We have no women.

You're a sorry lot, then.

We are a sorry lot, sir.

Well, I can't get you women.

I assumed as much, sir.

What are you going to do without women, then?

We will suffer, sir. And then we'll die out one by one.

Can any of you sing?

Yes, sir, we have many fine singers among us.

Order them to begin singing immediately.

Either women will find you this way or you will die

comforted. Meanwhile busy yourselves

with the meaningful tasks you have set for yourselves.

Sir, we will not rest until the babes arrive.

Family Sorrow

I was alone in the house reading the evening
paper and sipping a glass of sherry when a note
arrived by courier informing me that my brother
had been hospitalized. He had fallen from his
horse and was paralyzed. This struck me as funny
on two accounts: 1. I have no brother, and 2.
he has no horse. Nonetheless, I changed into my
tragic suit and quickly caught a taxi. At the
hospital "my brother" looked awful, but was exceed-
ingly happy to see me. I kissed him on the brow
and struggled to hold back tears. After a brief
chat, the nurse came in and injected him with some-
thing that made him turn green. "For the pain,"
she assured me. He began to smell like Walt
Whitman, so I crawled home, pausing only to sniff
at passing dogs and policemen.

An Afternoon in Hell

He cries awhile, for no apparent reason.
Sniffs, blows his nose. Then goes about his
business, stomp, pound, smash, crush, explode.
Then cries a little more, sob, blubber, bleat.
It's awful, he says. It's of no use. He throws
his chair through the window. It's a mess, he says.
The whole damned thing is useless. Now he's
really weeping, cascades, waterfalls, rivers.
I shouldn't bother, he says. It's a big, miserable
waste of time. His wife walks in. Honey,
haven't you finished changing the baby yet?

     Almost finished, he chirps.

Memory

A little bookstore used to call to me.
Eagerly I would go to it
hungry for news
and the sure friendship.
It never failed to provide me
with whatever I needed.
Bookstore with a donkey in its heart,
bookstore full of clouds and
sometimes lightning, showers.
Books just in from Australia,
books by madmen and giants.
Toucans would alight on my stovepipe hat
and solve mysteries with a few chosen words.
Picasso would appear in a kimono
requesting a discount, and then
laugh at his own joke.
Little bookstore with its belly
full of wisdom and confetti,
with eyebrows of wildflowers—
and customers from Denmark and Japan,
New York and California, psychics
and lawyers, clergymen and hitchhikers,
the wan, the strong, the crazy,
all needing books, needing directions,
needing a friend, or a place to sit down.

But then one day the shelves began to empty
and a hush fell over the store.
No new books arrived.
When the dying was done,
only a fragile, tattered thing remained,
and I haven't the heart to name it.

Mental-Health Workers

Mostly we were able to ignore the hairy thing
in the corner. It seemed to be leaking some green
fluid, but we could walk around that. It gave off
an unpleasant odor, a cross between Limburger cheese
and a decomposing skunk, but we never mentioned it.
It wasn't really hurting anybody. And then one day
I thought I heard it singing. And another day it
seemed to say I love you. And then one day it wasn't
there anymore, not lost but gone before.

Behind the Milk Bottle

is a crust of bread and three dead ladybugs,
also a flashlight and some Band-Aids.
In case of a power outage I'm all set.
Rubbing two dead ladybugs together
creates a bluish green light
by which one can enjoy the crust of bread
and forget about the hurricane or whatever.
I keep an extra in case one explodes.
Once as a river of molten lava
poured through my living room
I was cut off from my emergency kit,
my Band-Aids and so on, and had to crawl
out the window and go around.
The kitchen floor was like a frying pan,
so I sprung through the air and grabbed
my stuff and then went back around
and crawled back into the living room window,
though in this case it turned out
I never employed the items in my kit
as the lava ceased in less than a week.
As for pillagers, think twice:
behind the milk bottle is another milk bottle
and a nest of unruly ribbons
and a ghost who barks at airplanes.

Thinking Ahead to Possible Options and a Worst-Case Scenario

I swerved to avoid hitting a squirrel
in the center of the road and that's when
the deer came charging out of the forest
and forced me to hit the brakes for all I
was worth and I careened back to the other
side of the road just as a skunk came toddling
out of Mrs. Bancroft's front yard and I swung
back perhaps just grazing it a bit. I glanced
quickly in the rearview mirror and in that
instant a groundhog waddled from the side
of the road and I zigzagged madly and don't
know if I nipped it or not because up ahead I
could see a coyote stalking the Colliers'
cat. Oh well, I said, and drove the
rest of the way home without incident.

Boom-Boom

A man and a woman meet in an alley. They kiss
but they don't really know one another. You smell
like violets, he says, putting his hand on her breast.
You're strong, she says, rubbing herself on his thigh.
He runs his hands through her hair and pulls her tighter
to him. I must have you, he says. Yes, I want to
make love to you, she says, touching him between his
legs. Yes, you must give up your treasure to fruc-
tify the crops, he says. Oh yes, I want to fructify
very much, she says. The crops, I mean.

Hotel of the Golden Dawn

It was clear to us that the real owners
of the hotel were spiders. They were everywhere
but you had to look carefully. They had ingenious
ways of disguising themselves, except for the
clerk at the check-in desk. He was clearly a
spider, a pale pink translucent spider, a kindly
one. In fact, in my experience, all the spiders
in the hotel were benevolent. One stroked my
brow as I lay in bed trying to sleep. Another
kept flies off of my eggs in the morning. Many
of the guests I saw in the lobby seemed to me
inhuman, or at least toothless and drained of
their blood. It was a convention of some kind,
button makers, astronomers, comedians, florists,
prison guards, lamplighters, editors, whatever,
and they were having a very good time. The desk-
spider and the door-spider eyed them proudly.

Toads Talking by a River

A book can move from room to room
without anyone touching it. It can climb
the staircase and hide under the bed. It
can crawl into bed with you because it knows
you need company. And it can read to you
in your sleep and you wake a smarter person
or a sadder person. It is good to live
surrounded by books because you never know
what can happen next: lost in the inter-
stellar space between teacups in the cupboard,
found in the beak of a downy woodpecker,
the lovers staring into the void and then
jumping over it, flying into their beautiful
tomorrows like the heroes of a storm.

My Private Tasmania

has never been discovered,

is thought to be the source of all fire,

is a pigpen for the soul,

changes its shape and location

when you try to think of it.

It smells like a funeral parlor

full of orchids and makes you

want to run for your life.

And at the same time it's sexual,

salacious, creating a terrible hunger.

My Tasmania conceals beneath her

raven-black apron hundreds of

unknown species of wild pigs.

It rocks in the wind at night

and hums a beautiful melody.

Even the birds can't sleep

and begin to sing extinct songs.

Snakes are counting their worry beads.

I'm walking in circles,

getting closer and closer.

Walls of the coal mine

that is my head begin to cave in, crashing

in huge chunks to the floor,

shocking the bats out of their dreams

and the rats out of gnawing

on one another. Closer, I said,

I must be getting closer.

The smell of rotting flesh

was gagging me. I couldn't see
through the smoke and haze.
I stop circling, begin to laugh.
My mother says, "Jimmy, please
stop laughing, you're frightening us."

No Explanation

Down the street they are pulverizing the old
police station. They started by crushing it,
then they beat it, and then they proceeded to
grind it up. I walked by it just a few minutes
ago. All that's left is a mountain of woodchips. . . .
"Where are the policemen?" I asked one of the
workers. He pointed to the mountain of woodchips
and said, "We never saw them." I walked on
thinking about Officer Plotkin, how he'd arrested
me when I was guilty, and how he'd come to my aid
when I'd needed him. I stopped and looked back
over my shoulder. I longed to be arrested,
to be saved.

The London Times

We had walked several hours from our hotel
to find Queen Mary's Garden. Roses were in full
bloom as far as we could see, hundreds of varieties
of roses. The fragrances mingling in the air were
intoxicating. A pond reflected the roses along
its banks. All the variations of peach, pink,
red, yellow and white were inflaming our vision.
It is widely rumored that the current Queen pees
a little on each rose every morning.

You Think You Know a Woman

I am thinking of her almond breath
and her irrefutable impact on orthodox mathematics
and physics as well. She's also a spider,
of some sort, and a little bit of vanilla pudding.
Her soft curves, her beehives, her waterfalls
and deserts also cross my mind, as well as her
narcotics and magnolias, her sables and minks
and fumigations, as well as her oracles and demarcations.
How many comets has she actually seen?
I don't know. But I do know her favorite spots in
Delaware, and her mystery play, her radar, her shorthand.
Her gift as a topiarist and her dew point.
Her carrots and mangoes and chimney sweeps.
She saved a rock about to fall from a ledge.
She found some socks thrown into a corner.

Chirpy, the Ruffian

We were on our way out to the beach
to visit some whales we had gotten to know
slightly when the car suddenly exploded.
Mercifully, we were spared, or some of us
were spared anyway. Bodo looked as sharp
as ever, like a smoky Egyptian cat eager
to be fed. Perhaps some terrorist had
gotten to us, God knows we have made our
fair share of enemies! We were the Sand People,
we ate sand. The wind blew right through
us and we kept walking, kept falling down.

Snake-Charming Secrets of the Indian Subcontinent

I was seated at the bar having my usual
five o'clock cocktail, a martini. It had been
a hellish day at the office and I was trying to
shake off some of the tension. "Can I have your
olive?" the stranger sitting next to me asked.
"Hell, no," I answered testily. "Well, then, can
I have a sip, I've never tasted a martini."
"Get your own," I said. That shut him up. I
went back to my thoughts. The boss was driving
me too hard, maybe looking for an excuse to
let me go. I wouldn't be the first. I stared
into the mirror behind the bar. The man next
to me looked truly wretched. "What's your
problem, pal?" I said to him. "You're not
eating your olive," he said.

Doink

I am a scientist who don't know nothing
yet. But every morning I peer into my micro-
scope to see if any wee thing be swimming
around. (Once I thought I saw a dog of some
kind.) And every night I look through my
telescope to see if anything's fluttering or
sputtering in the sky (I've spotted several
stars and named them all after me, Prince
Hubertus zu Lowenstein). In the afternoons
I read ladies' fashion magazines. They sharpen
my mind and give me many of my best ideas.
When my wife, the Princess, sees me in my
latest outfit she always says, "Cowabunga!"
several times.

Somehow Not Aware That She Was Heaven-Born

The sun was shining through the rain
thus creating the effect of a second coming
not of Christ but of some eerie one-eyed
beast, bodiless save for the eye, which in
itself is bleary and sad. A thunderclap
scared me half to death. I was just sitting
in my chair growing a beard, my brain lit up
like a pinball machine and I prayed for order.
Yolanda asked me if I wanted a sandwich.
"A sandwich is perhaps our only hope, our
best hope, our last chance to survive this
big blow. You are a saint and a genius,
Yolanda," I said. "Get it yourself," she
said.

A Children's Story About an Anemic Bedbug

The man sitting next to me on the airplane
said he was an international arms dealer. He also
said that he had written poetry in his youth and
that it had made him very happy and that he wasn't
quite sure why he had quit it and how he had ended
up doing what he does now. I got the impression
that he dealt with some pretty unsavory characters,
dictators, terrorists, the bottom scum of humanity.
He was obviously very wealthy, but lived with a
certain degree of fear and dread. I offered him
a mint and he scrutinized it as if it might be laced
with belladonna. He looked me straight in the eyes
and then with a certain amount of shame took it
and thanked me. I put the mints back into my
breast pocket without taking one myself. That's
when he took out his handkerchief and spat the mint
discreetly into it. We sat there in silence for a
long time, slowly turning to ash on a windswept
wilderness.

To Each His Own

When Joey returned from the war he worked
on his motorcycle in the garage most days. A
few of his old buddies were still around—Bobby
and Scooter—and once or twice a week they'd
go down to the club and have a few beers. But
Joey never talked about the war. He had a
tattoo on his right hand that said DEVI and he
wouldn't even tell what that meant. Months
passed and Joey showed no interest in getting
a job. His old Indian motorcycle ran like a
top, it gleamed, it purred. One night at dinner
he shocked us all by saying, "Devi's coming to
live with us. It's going to be difficult. She's
an elephant."

Burnt Green Earth

He was a bold little tyke even at the age
of three. He would have fought bulls if given
half a chance. He would have robbed trains.
He would have rescued women from waterfalls.
He ate like a full-grown glutton, and when he
was finished all the walls and floors of the
house were covered with food he'd flung for the
joy of it. He was so fast on his feet his mother
and father could never catch him. He found
everything immensely funny, even falling down
staircases. He was always proud of his wounds.
His parents seemed exhausted all the time. They
looked terrible. When they finally fell asleep
at night the child would climb out of his bed
and work on his novel about the frailty of the
human race and the unwhisperable starry night sky.

All Over the Lot

We were at the ball game when a small child
came up to me and thwacked me in my private area.
He turned and walked away without a single word.
I was in horrible pain for a couple of minutes,
then I went looking for the rascal. When I
found him he was holding his mother's hand and
looking like the picture of innocence. "Is that
your son?" I asked of the lady. She shot me a
look that could fry eggs, and then she slapped
me really hard. "Mind your own business," she
screaked. The boy grinned up at me. My old
tweed vest was infested with fleas. I started
walking backwards. People were shoving me this
way and that. To each I replied, "God, I love
this game, I love this game."

Negative Employee Situation

The Huntingtons had a live-in maid
by the name of Mary. Mary was very religious
and prayed a good deal of the time. In fact,
as the years went by Mary pretty much ceased
working altogether and prayed all of the time.
Mrs. Huntington cooked for her and cleaned her
room as well as the rest of the house. Mr.
Huntington would never rebuke Mary because
he believed her prayers benefited the whole
household. The Huntingtons were not themselves
religious, but they were superstitious. And
when Mary died after a short illness, they hired
another Mary, but this one cleaned and scrubbed
and vacuumed and dusted and polished and cooked.
The Huntingtons were terrified for their lives
and discussed plans for killing the new Mary.

The Lack of Good Qualities

Granny sat drinking a bourbon and branch water
by the picture window. It was early evening and she
had finished the dinner dishes and put them away and
now it was her time to do as she pleased. "All my
children are going to hell, and my grandchildren, too,"
she said to me, one of her children. She took a long
slug of her drink and sighed. One of her eyes was all
washed out, the result of some kind of dueling accident
in her youth. That and the three black hairs on her
chin which she refused to cut kept the grandchildren
at a certain distance. "Be a sweetheart and get me
another drink, would you, darling?" I make her a really
strong one. "I miss the War, I really do. But your
granddaddy was such a miserable little chickenshit he
managed to come back alive. Can you imagine that? And
him wearing all those medals, what a joke! And so I
had to kill him, I had no choice. I poisoned the son
of a bitch and got away with it. And so I ask you, who's
the real hero?" "You are, Granny," I said, knowing I was
going to hell if only to watch her turn to stone.

Climbing Like a Monkey Through the Thick Branches

It was late at night and someone was singing
outside my living room window. I reached for the
hatchet under the cushion on my couch. It sounded
like "I Only Have Eyes for You," which was very
frightening, directly threatening my existence.
I turned all the lights off and tripped over the dog.
The hatchet got stuck in the floor and I had a hell
of a time wedging it loose, nearly lodging it in
my forehead. The voice went on singing, a lovely
voice of the female persuasion. A voice like my
mother's. I clutched the hatchet tighter and held
it over my head. In utter darkness I was slowly
dancing in circles and humming along with the tune.

The Plumber

When the plumber arrived to fix the water
heater he eyed me with considerable suspicion. I
told him how grateful I was that he had come
and he actually growled at me. I asked him if
I could get him something to drink and he said,
"I don't want your stinking water." I pointed
him to the basement door and he spat at me
saying, "What do you think I'm an idiot?" Then
I heard pounding and cursing from the basement
for the next forty-five minutes. I considered
calling the police, but knew they wouldn't
believe me. I considered getting in my car and
just getting the hell out of there. As he came
up the steps I could hear him whimpering, actual-
ly sobbing. He opened the door and threw his
arms around me. "I can't fix it!" he said. "I'm
a terrible plumber!" I held him in my arms and
we rocked back and forth with me gently patting
him on the back. A little while after he was
able to leave, his wife called to ask if he was
alright. I said that he was just fine and she
thanked me very sweetly.

Like a Manta Ray

I can swim the length of the public pool
underwater. I like to swim right along the
bottom with my eyes open, and sometimes I find
things—a barrette, some change, a ring, a gold
chain, some plastic spacemen, a comb, nothing
too extraordinary. But this one day I was
swimming along and I spotted a pearl, and then
another and so on until I had both hands full
of pearls, real pearls. When I surfaced I
heard this darkly tanned, obviously wealthy woman
screaming at the pool attendant, "Someone has
stolen my pearls!" I quickly put the pearls inside
the netting of my swimming suit and climbed out
of the pool. I walked quickly toward the
dressing room, but then one pearl, then two, then
a third slipped out from my trunks and bounced
across the poolside toward a three-year-old boy
who had been listening to the lady with amusement.
He put his finger over his lips and smiled at me.
I had no use for the pearls and didn't want them,
but somehow at that moment I didn't want her
to have them anymore.

The Old Candy, the New Candy

Candy was primping in front of the mirror
for what seemed like an hour. I said, "We're
going to be late. You look great." She said,
"My hair's all wrong. It looks like I have
mice living in it." I said, "It looks the
way it always looks." She said, "I know,
and only now did I realize mice are living
in it." I said, "Mice are nice, I like mice."
"Where are the scissors?" she said, "I'm going
to cut it all off." "NO," I said, "you can't
do that." She found the scissors and started
cutting. I was horrified, but I couldn't
stop her. She cut and cut and cut, beautiful
tresses falling on the bathroom floor. One
mouse narrowly escaped having its tail clipped,
two others didn't fare as well. I never men-
tioned any of this to Candy, who was too busy
shearing herself. I hid my tears, too.

Mob of Good Old Boys

Why do people go to the theater and
laugh all the way through the really sad films?
This happens to me all the time and I hate
it because I like to cry through the really sad films
and it's hard to cry when somebody is laugh-
ing that loudly. Maybe they like to see
people suffer because they're animals and
it's not them. It makes me so mad I want
to punch them out. I mean, what's so funny
about a little boy dying or a dog getting
run over or even a hamster going up in
smoke or a mob killing Frankenstein's so-called monster, I
mean, that is really not one bit funny.
I even named my dog Frankenstein and I
cry every time I see him or think
of him. He is always trying to console me
but it never works. Life is as fragile
and as beautiful as a spiderweb and the
wind is blowing, always blowing.

A Tattered Bible Stuffed with Memos

I stood at the southwest window for
a long time just staring out at the field
and empty road. A hawk on the telephone
line studied the field for any sign of move-
ment, then eventually he swooped down and
had his snack. A tractor pulling a wagon-
load of hay has crept over the hill. Five teen-
agers in a green convertible passed him at
a great speed and disappeared behind a cloud
of dust. A storm was rolling in, I could
feel the barometer dropping. This is where
the chicken catches the ax.

The Bookclub

Bobbie came home from her bookclub
completely drunk and disheveled. Three
buttons from her blouse were missing and
she had scratches down both cheeks. "Jesus,"
I said, "what the hell happened to you?"
"They all hated that book," she said, "you
know, that one that had me crying all last
week, about the girl's mother dying, and
then her baby getting sick and her husband
leaving her. They said it was corny, and
I just couldn't take it. I couldn't sit
there and make fun of that poor
woman." "So what happened?" I said. "Well,
Irene was laughing and that's when I got up
and slapped her. And she punched me in the
gut and I grabbed her hair and threw her to
the floor and kicked her in the face. And
then Rosie and Tina and that bitch Sonia
from Leverett all jumped on me and punched
me a hundred times and I didn't know what
was happening." "So when did you get drunk?"
I asked. "Oh, when it was all over we went
out to Lucky 7 together and laughed and
laughed about it." "A bunch of tough broads,"
I said. "Nah, they're all pussycats," she
said, looking badly in need of repair.

The Painter of the Night

Someone called in a report that she had
seen a man painting in the dark over by the
pond. A police car was dispatched to go in-
vestigate. The two officers with their big
flashlights walked all around the pond, but
found nothing suspicious. Hatcher was the
younger of the two, and he said to Johnson,
"What do you think he was painting?" Johnson
looked bemused and said, "The dark, stupid.
What else could he have been painting?" Hatcher,
a little hurt, said, "Frogs in the Dark, Lily
Pads in the Dark, Pond in the Dark. Just as
many things exist in the dark as they do in
the light." Johnson paused, exasperated. Then
Hatcher added, "I'd like to see them. Hell,
I might even buy one. Maybe there's more out
there than we know. We are the police, after
all. We need to know."

The Eternal Ones of the Dream

I was walking down this dirt road out
in the country. It was a sunny day in early
fall. I looked up and saw this donkey pulling
a cart coming toward me. There was no driver
nor anyone leading the donkey so far as I could
see. The donkey was just moping along. When
we met the donkey stopped and I scratched its
snout in greeting and it seemed grateful. It
seemed like a very lonely donkey, but what
donkey wouldn't feel alone on the road like that?
And then it occurred to me to see what, if anything,
was in the cart. There was only a black box,
or a coffin, about two feet long and a foot wide.
I started to lift the lid, but then I didn't.
I couldn't. I realized that this donkey was on
some woeful mission, who knows where, to the ends
of the earth, so I gave him an apple, scratched
his nose a last time and waved him on, little
man that I was.

Boobies of Fernando Po

We stopped at a tag sale and there was
a blender that I was considering. The owner
walked up to me and I asked him if it worked.
"Sure, it works," he said. "If it works so
good how come you want to get rid of it?" I
asked him. He told me they had got a new one.
And I said, "Why would you get a new one if
this one still works?" "Upgrading," he said.
"So you think you're too good for this blender,
but it's just right for me, is that it?" I
said. "Listen, buddy, if you don't want the
blender it's fine by me, okay?" "So you don't
want my money, my money's not good enough for
you?" "Just take the blender and go," he said.
"So now you're giving me, a complete stranger,
a gift of this perfectly good blender?" I said.
My wife was tugging at my arm. "Come on, honey,"
she said, "this man's crazy, let's go." Back
in the car, I said, "I guess we showed him who's
boss." "You sure did," my wife said. "Even
free that blender was much too expensive." I
thought that over for a moment. "Didn't Nietzsche
say that?" I asked, swerving to miss a pig
in the road.

The Magic Flight

A horse broke out of the Saunders' pen.
It was a beautiful black gelding, not too large.
It made it to the highway and was galloping down
the center of it for all its might, cars swerving
all over the road, some screeching to a halt, others
narrowly missing one another. The police were called,
and three cars were sent, sirens blaring, lights
flashing, creating yet another hazard. It was chaos
out there, and the horse seemed tireless. The police
got out enough in front of the horse to set up a
roadblock, and the horse jumped right over the police
cars as if that were the most natural thing in the
world for a horse to do, and I suppose it is. They
called for more help and there was more chaos on the
road. It basically wasn't safe to be on that road
unless you were that horse. Now there were five
police cars chasing the horse. One truck had toppled
over and several cars had crashed into one another,
though no one was seriously hurt. As nightfall
approached they still hadn't caught the horse. It
seems it had left the highway, but no one had any
idea which way it had gone. When questioned by
reporters, the police spokesman said he wasn't sure if
it was a horse or just a case of mass hysteria.
The Saunders said they never had a horse like that
or, at least, if they did they didn't know it.

The Diagnosis

Lincoln was sixty years old when the
doctor told him he only had forty more years
to live. He didn't tell his wife, in whom
he confided everything, or any of his friends,
because this new revelation made him feel all
alone in a way he had never experienced before.
He and Rachel had been inseparable for as long
as he could remember and he thought that if she
knew the prognosis she would begin to feel alone,
too. But Rachel could see the change in him
and within a couple of days she figured out
what it meant. "You're dying," she said, "aren't
you?" "Yes, I'm dying," Lincoln said, "I only
have forty years." "I feel you drifting away
from me already," she said. "It's the drifting
that kills you," Lincoln whispered.

Kinky's Head

"Would you like to have your head examined?"
I said to Kinky, who was holding his head. "Oh yes,"
he said, "I would like to know what's wrong with
me." Gloom was his life, despair was his only food.
I opened up his head. My God, it was dark in there,
and full of cobwebs with dead flies in them. "There
are no lights in here," I said. "It looks like you
have had no visitors in years. And there's not a
trace of an idea, just a rat gnawing on its tail
hoping to become a saint in some counterfeit hell."
"I love the rat," Kinky said. "He's the last of
my monsters, old skin and bones."

The Flying Petunias

When I let the cat in I didn't see
that it had a mouse in its mouth. But then
it set the mouse down on the kitchen floor
and they proceeded to play cat and mouse.
How very apt, I thought. The mouse stood about
one foot from the cat and the cat would extend
one leg slowly and touch the mouse on its head.
The mouse would sort of bow in supplication.
Then the mouse would dash on and snuggle up
under the cat's belly. One time the mouse
ran up the cat's back and sat on the crook
of her neck, and the cat seemed calmly proud
to have it there. They kept me entertained
like this for about an hour, but then it
started to irritate me that they had this
all worked out so well and I threw the cat
out. The mouse ran under the kitchen sink.
I let kitty in when it was our bedtime.
She has her pillow and I have mine and we've
always slept very sweetly together. In the
middle of this night, however, I feel these
tiny feet creeping across my neck and onto
my chin. I open my eyes slowly and kitty
is staring at me from her pillow and I am
staring at her. Then I close my eyes and
she closes hers and we all three dream of
joining the circus.

Capital Punishment

No one was allowed to know the name of
the town executioner, and he wore a mask at
all times. If we spotted him doing his errands
in town, grocery shopping or whatever, we would
follow him and taunt him. "Hey, Mr. Executioner,
how many have you whacked today?" He's not allowed
to speak back to us, so we figure we really get
under his skin. We don't really dislike him,
it's just his job after all. We don't really know
who gives him his orders, some committee probably.
Mr. Executioner is married to Mrs. Executioner
and she too must wear a mask at all times, and
their children wear masks as well. They don't
even know who they are.

Memoir of the Hawk

I was sitting on a bench in the park when
I saw this large hawk circling overhead. I had
my eyes on it when it suddenly swooped down and
picked up this little baby right out of its
carriage and flew away with it. My heart almost
stopped beating. I ran over to the mother, who
was eyeing a dress in a window. "Ma'am," I
stuttered, "that bird just stole your baby. . . ."
She looked into the carriage and then up at the
sky. "Oh, I know that bird. She's a good bird.
She just took my baby to play with her babies
for a while. She'll bring him back in a short
time. My baby loves her babies. But thanks for
telling me. By the way, what do you think of
this dress? Is it right for me?" I thought of
her baby sailing through the sky in the claws
of that bird. "Well," I said, "I think the
mignonette green captures the amplitude of your
inner aviary." "What are you, some kind of loose
nutcase? Get out of here before I call the
police," she said.

Rapture

"If you sit here a long time and are real
quiet, you just might get to see one of those
blue antelope," I said to Cora. "I'd do any-
thing to see a blue antelope," she said. "I'd
take off all my clothes and lie completely still
in the grass all day." "That's a good idea,"
I said, "taking off the clothes, I mean, it's
more natural." I'd met Cora in the library the
night before and had told her about the blue
antelope, so we'd made a date to try and see
them. We lay naked next to one another for hours.
It was a beautiful, sunny day with a breeze that
tickled. Finally, Cora whispered into my ear,
"My God, I see them. They're so delicate, so
graceful. They're like angels, cornflower
angels." I looked at Cora. She was disappearing.
She was becoming one of them.

RETURN TO THE CITY OF WHITE DONKEYS

Long-Term Memory

I was sitting in the park feeding pigeons
when a man came over to me and scrutinized my
face right up close. "There's a statue of you
over there," he said. "You should be dead. What
did you do to deserve a statue?" "I've never seen
a statue of me," I said. "There can't be a statue
of me. I've never done anything to deserve a
statue. And I'm definitely not dead." "Well,
go look for yourself. It's you alright, there's
no mistaking that," he said. I got up and walked
over where it was. It was me alright. I looked
like I was gazing off into the distance, or the
future, like those statues of pioneers. It didn't
have my name on it or anything, but it was me.
A lady came up to me and said, "You're looking at
your own statue. Isn't that against the law, or
something?" "It should be," I said, "but this is
my first offense. Maybe they'll let me off light."
"It's against nature, too," she said, "and bad
manners, I think." "I couldn't agree with you
more," I said. "I'm walking away right now, sorry."
I went back to my bench. The man was sitting there.
"Maybe you're a war hero. Maybe you died in the
war," he said. "Never been a soldier," I said.
"Maybe you founded this town three hundred years
ago," he said. "Well, if I did, I don't remember

it now," I said. "That's a long time ago," he
said, "you coulda forgot." I went back to feeding
the pigeons. Oh, yes, founding the town. It was
coming back to me now. It was on a Wednesday.
A light rain, my horse slowed . . .

The Memories of Fish

Stanley took a day off from the office
and spent the whole day talking to fish in
his aquarium. To the little catfish scuttling
along the bottom he said, "Vacuum that scum,
boy. Suck it up, that's your job." The skinny
pencil fish swam by and he said, "Scribble,
scribble, scribble. Write me a novel, needle-
nose." The angel executed a particularly
masterful left turn and Stanley said, "You're
no angel, but you sure can drive." Then he broke
for lunch and made himself a tuna fish sandwich,
the irony of which did not escape him. Oh no,
he wallowed in it, savoring every bite. Then
he returned to his chair in front of the aquarium.
A swarm of tiny neons amused him. "What do you
think this is, Times Square!" he shouted. And
so it went long into the night. The next morning
Stanley was horribly embarrassed by his behavior
and he apologized to the fish several times,
but they never really forgave him. He had mocked
their very fishiness, and for this there can be
no forgiveness.

It Happens Like This

I was outside St. Cecilia's Rectory
smoking a cigarette when a goat appeared beside me.
It was mostly black and white, with a little reddish
brown here and there. When I started to walk away,
it followed. I was amused and delighted, but wondered
what the laws were on this kind of thing. There's
a leash law for dogs, but what about goats? People
smiled at me and admired the goat. "It's not my goat,"
I explained. "It's the town's goat. I'm just taking
my turn caring for it." "I didn't know we had a goat,"
one of them said. "I wonder when my turn is." "Soon,"
I said. "Be patient. Your time is coming." The goat
stayed by my side. It stopped when I stopped. It looked
up at me and I stared into its eyes. I felt he knew
everything essential about me. We walked on. A police-
man on his beat looked us over. "That's a mighty
fine goat you got there," he said, stopping to admire.
"It's the town's goat," I said. "His family goes back
three hundred years with us," I said, "from the beginning."
The officer leaned forward to touch him, then stopped
and looked up at me. "Mind if I pat him?" he asked.
"Touching this goat will change your life," I said.
"It's your decision." He thought real hard for a minute,
and then stood up and said, "What's his name?" "He's
called the Prince of Peace," I said. "God! This town
is like a fairy tale. Everywhere you turn there's mystery
and wonder. And I'm just a child playing cops and robbers

forever. Please forgive me if I cry." "We forgive you, Officer," I said. "And we understand why you, more than anybody, should never touch the Prince." The goat and I walked on. It was getting dark and we were beginning to wonder where we would spend the night.

The Florist

I realized Mother's Day was just two days
away, so I went to the florist and said, "I'd
like to send my mother a dozen long-stem red
roses." The guy looked at me and said, "My mother's
dead." I thought this was slightly unprofessional
of him, so I said, "How much would that be?" He
wiped his eyes and said, "Oh, that's alright. I'm
over it, really. She never loved me anyway, so why
should I grieve." "Can they be delivered by Thursday?"
I inquired. "She hated flowers," he said. "I've
never known a woman to hate flowers the way she did.
She wanted me to be a dentist, like her father.
Can you imagine that, torturing people all day.
Instead, I give them pleasure. She disowned me,
really. And yet I miss her," and then he started
crying again. I gave him my handkerchief and he
blew his nose heartily into it. My annoyance had
given way to genuine pity. This guy was a mess.
I didn't know what to do. Finally I said, "Listen,
why don't you send a dozen roses to my mother. You
can tell her you are a friend of mine. My mother
loves flowers, and she'll love you for sending them
to her." He stopped crying and scowled at me. "Is
this some kind of trick? A trap or something, to
get me tied up in a whole other mother thing, because
if it is, I mean, I just got rid of one, and I can't
take it, another I mean, I'm not as strong as I
appear. . . ." "Forget it," I said, "it was a bad idea,

and I'm certainly not sending my mother any flowers
this year, that, too, was a bad idea. Will you be
alright if I leave now, I have other errands, but
if you need me I can stay." "Yes, if you could stay
with me awhile. My name is Skeeter and Mother's
Day is always such a trial for me. I miss her more
every passing day," he said. And so we sat there
holding hands for an hour or so, and then I was on
my way to the cleaners, the bank and the gas station.

Lost River

Jill and I had been driving for hours
on these little back country roads and we hadn't
seen another car or a store of any kind in all
that time. We were trying to get to a village
called Lost River and we were running out of gas.
There was a man there that owns a pterodactyl
wing and we heard that he might want to sell it.
He was tired of it, we were told. Finally, I see
an old pickup truck coming up behind us and I
pull over and get out of the car and wave. The
man starts to pass us by, but changes his mind
and stops. I ask him if he knows how to get to Lost
River and he says he's never heard of it, but
can give us directions to the closest town called
Last Grocery Store. I thank him and we eventually
find Last Grocery Store, which consists of three
trailers and a little bitsy grocery store. The
owner is old and nearly blind, but he's glad to
meet us and we're glad to meet him. I ask him
if he knows how to get to Lost River from here.
He ponders for a while, and then says, "I don't
see how you could get there, unless you're walking.
There's no road out in them parts. Why would
anybody be wanting to go to Lost River, there's
nothing there." "There's a man there that's got
a pterodactyl wing he might be willing to sell,"
I say. "Hell, I'll sell you mine. I can't see
it anymore, so I might as well sell it," he says.

Jill and I look at each other, incredulous. "Well
we'd sure like to see it," I say. "No problem,"
he says, "I keep it right here in the back of the store."
He brings it out and it's beautiful, delicate
and it's real, I'm certain of it. The foot even
has its claws on it. We're speechless and rather
terrified of holding it, though he hands it to us
trustingly. My whole body feels like it's vibrating,
like I'm a harp of time. I'm sort of embarrassed,
but finally I ask him how much he wants for it.
"Oh, just take it. It always brought me luck, but
I've had all the luck I need," he says. Jill gives
him a kiss on the cheek and I shake his hand and
thank him. Tomorrow: Lost River.

Lust for Life

Veronica has the best apartment in town.
It's on the third story and has big plate glass
windows that look straight down on the town common.
She has a bird's-eye view of all the protesters,
the fairs, the lovers, people eating lunch on
park benches; in general, the lifeblood of the
town. The more Veronica watched all these little
dramas, the less desire she had to actually go
out and be one herself. I called her from time
to time, but her conversation consisted of her
descriptions of what was going on in the common.
"Now he's kissing her and saying good-bye. He's
getting on the bus. The bus is pulling out.
Wait a minute, she's just joined hands with
another guy. I can't believe it! These people
are behaving like trash. There's a real tiny
old lady with a walker trying to go into the
bookstore, but she keeps stopping and looking
over her shoulder. She thinks she's being
followed." "Veronica," I say. "I'm dying."
"Two of the richest and nastiest lawyers in
town are arguing over by the drinking fountain.
They're actually shouting, I can almost hear
them. Oh my god, one of them has shoved the
other. It's incredible, Artie. You should be
here," she says. "War has been declared with
England, Veronica. Have you heard that?" I
say. "That's great, Artie," she says. "Remember

the girl who kissed the guy getting on the bus
and then immediately took up with the other guy?
Well, now she's flirting with the parking officer
and he's loving it and flirting back with her.
He just tore up a ticket he had written for her.
I'm really beginning to like this girl after all."
"That's great, Veronica," I say. "Why don't
you check and see if your little panties are
on fire yet," and I hang up, and I don't think
she even notices. I wonder if I'm supposed to
be worried about her. But in the end I don't.
Veronica has the best apartment in town.

Banking Rules

I was standing in line at the bank and
the fellow in front of me was humming. The
line was long and slow, and after a while
the humming began to irritate me. I said to
the fellow, "Excuse me, would you mind not
humming." And he said, "Was I humming?
I'm sorry, I didn't realize it." And he went
right on humming. I said, "Sir, you're
humming again." "Me, humming?" he said.
"I don't think so." And then he went on
humming. I was about to blow my lid. Instead,
I went to find the manager. I said, "See
that man over there in the blue suit?" "Yes,"
he said, "what about him?" "He won't stop
humming." I said. "I've asked him politely
several times, but he won't stop." "There's
no crime in humming," he said. I went back
and took my place in line. I listened, but
there was nothing coming out of him. I said,
"Are you okay, pal?" He looked mildly peeved,
and gave me no reply. I felt myself shrinking.
The manager of the bank walked briskly up
to me and said, "Sir, are you aware of the
fact that you're shrinking?" I said I was.
And he said, "I'm afraid we don't allow that
kind of behavior in this bank. I have to ask
you to leave." The air was whistling out
of me, I was almost gone.

The Promotion

I was a dog in my former life, a very good
dog, and, thus, I was promoted to a human being.
I liked being a dog. I worked for a poor farmer
guarding and herding his sheep. Wolves and coyotes
tried to get past me almost every night, and not
once did I lose a sheep. The farmer rewarded me
with good food, food from his table. He may have
been poor, but he ate well. And his children
played with me, when they weren't in school or
working in the field. I had all the love any dog
could hope for. When I got old, they got a new
dog, and I trained him in the tricks of the trade.
He quickly learned, and the farmer brought me into
the house to live with them. I brought the farmer
his slippers in the morning, as he was getting
old, too. I was dying slowly, a little bit at a
time. The farmer knew this and would bring the
new dog in to visit me from time to time. The
new dog would entertain me with his flips and
flops and nuzzles. And then one morning I just
didn't get up. They gave me a final burial down
by the stream under a shade tree. That was the
end of my being a dog. Sometimes I miss it so
I sit by the window and cry. I live in a high-rise
that looks out at a bunch of other high-rises.
At my job I work in a cubicle and barely speak
to anyone all day. This is my reward for being
a good dog. The human wolves don't even see me.
They fear me not.

A Sound Like Distant Thunder

I had fallen asleep on the couch with the
TV on. Every now and then I would open an eye
and see someone get stabbed or eaten by a monster.
Once, a beautiful woman was taking off her blouse.
And then the phone rang. I couldn't tell if it
was a TV phone or my own. I sat up, half-asleep,
and reached for the phone. "Howie," a woman's
voice said, "is that you? You sound like you were
asleep." "I was," I said. I wasn't Howie, but
I was in the mood to talk to this woman. "Howie,
I miss you. I wish I were in bed with you right
now," she said. "I miss you, too. I wish you
were here with me right now," I said. I hated
not knowing her name, and I didn't even know if I could
call her "honey" or "sweetie" or any other endear-
ment. "Why don't you come over right now," I
said. "Oh you know I'm in Australia. And my
work here won't be done for another month. It's
just hell being away from you this long," she said.
"I love you," I said, and I think I meant it.
"You mean the world to me, Howie. I couldn't get
through this without knowing you love me. I think
of you all the time. I look at your picture
every chance I get. It's what gives me strength,
that and our brief phone calls. Now go back to
sleep and dream of me, dream of me kissing you
and holding you. I have to go now. I love you,
Howie," she said and hung up. And though my state

may be described as a gladdened stupor, I felt like a Howie, I really did, and I believed in my heart that the nameless, faceless one indentured in Australia really loved me, and that my great love for her gave her strength. I cozied up on the couch and fell into a sweet sleep. But then I heard a lion roar, and I feared for both of our lives. "Howie!" she cried. "Save me!" But I couldn't. I was busy elsewhere, tying my shoe.

Of Whom Am I Afraid?

I was feeling a little at loose ends, so
I went to the Farmer's Supply store and just
strolled up and down the aisles, examining
the merchandise, none of which was of any use
to me, but the feed sacks and seeds had a calm-
ing effect on me. At some point there was an
old, grizzled farmer standing next to me holding
a rake, and I said to him, "Have you ever read
much Emily Dickinson?" "Sure," he said, "I
reckon I've read all of her poems at least a
dozen times. She's a real pistol. And I've
even gotten into several fights about them
with some of my neighbors. One guy said she
was too 'prissy' for him. And I said, 'Hell,
she's tougher than you'll ever be.' When I
finished with him, I made him sit down and read
The Complete Poems over again, all 1,775 of them.
He finally said, 'You're right, Clyde, she's
tougher than I'll ever be.' And he was crying
like a baby when he said that." Clyde slapped
my cheek and headed toward the counter with
his new rake. I bought some ice tongs, which
made me surprisingly happy, and for which I
had no earthly use.

Silver Queen

I pulled my car over by the farmstand on
Northwest Street. "How's the corn this year?"
I asked the farmer. "It's the best ever," he
said. "You say that every year," I said. "No
I don't," he said. "Yes you do," I said. "No
I don't," he said. "Yes you do," I said. "I
don't," he said. "Well, you do," I said, "but
let's not make a federal case of it," I said.
"Fair enough," he said. "What kind you got?" I
asked. "Silver Queen," he said. "That's not
Silver Queen," I said. "I know Silver Queen
when I see it and that's not Silver Queen."
"Mister, I've been growing corn for forty-five
years. I know every damned thing there is about
growing corn. I can grow corn in my sleep.
I was growing corn before you were born, and
I'll probably keep right on growing corn after
I die," he said. "If you could stand to part
with a dozen ears of your beautiful Silver Queen,
I'd be much obliged," I said. That night, the
kids all said, "This is the best ever," and
I agreed. The next day I was driving down
Northwest Street again, and I stopped at the
stand and got out and said to the farmer,
"Please forgive me for doubting you. It's
some terrible flaw in me. You were right, it
was the best ever. My children thank you, my

wife thanks you, and I thank you more than
I can ever say," I said. "I forgive you, my
wife forgives you, and the corn forgives you,"
he said, sweeping his arm back toward his fields.
"Oh, yes," I said, "the corn, the corn . . ."

The Formal Invitation

I was invited to a formal dinner party given by Marguerite Farnish
Burridge and her husband, Knelm Oswald Lancelot Burridge. I
had never met either of them, and had no idea why I was invited.
When the butler announced me, Mrs. Burridge came up and greeted me
quite graciously. "I'm so happy you could join us," she said.
"I know Knelm is looking forward to talking to you later." "I
can't wait," I said, "I mean, the pleasure's all mine." Nothing
came out right. I wanted to escape right then, but Mrs. Burridge
dragged me and introduced me to some of her friends. "This is
Nicholas and Sondra Pepperdene. Nicholas is a spy," she said.
"I am not," he said. "Yes, you are, darling. Everyone knows it,"
she said. "And Sondra does something with swans, I'm not
sure what. She probably mates them, knowing Sondra." "Really!
I'm saving them from extinction," Mrs. Pepperdene said. "And this
is Mordecai Rhinelander, and, as you might guess from his name,
he's a Nazi. And his wife, Dagmar, is a Nazi, too. Still, lovely
people," she said. "Marguerite, you're giving our new friend
a very bad impression," Mr. Rhinelander said. "Oh, it's my party
and I can say what I want," Mrs. Burridge said. A servant was
passing with cocktails and she grabbed two off the tray and handed
me one. "I hope you like martinis," she said, and left me standing
there. "My name is Theodore Fullerton," I said, "and I'm a depraved
jazz musician. I prey on young women, take drugs whenever possible,
but most of the time I just sleep all day and am out of work."
They looked at one another, and then broke out laughing. I smiled
like an idiot and sipped my drink. I thought it was going to be

an awful party, but I just told the truth whenever I was spoken
to, and people thought I was hilariously funny. At dinner, I was
seated between Carmen Milanca and Godina Barnafi. The first course was
fresh crabmeat on a slice of kiwi. Mine managed to slip off the
plate and landed in the lap of Carmen Milanca. She had on a
very tight, short black dress. She smiled at me, waiting to see
what I would do. I reached over and plucked it from its nest.
"Nice shot," she said. "It was something of a bull's-eye, wasn't
it?" I said. Godina Barnafi asked me if I found wealthy women
to be sexy. "Oh yes, of course," I said, "but I generally prefer
poor, homeless waifs, you know, runaways, mentally addled,
unwashed, sickly, starving women." "Fascinating," she said. A leg of lamb
was served. Knelm Burridge proposed a toast. "To my good friends
gathered here tonight, and to your great achievements in the further-
ance of peace on Earth." I still had no idea what I was doing
there. I mentioned this to Carmen since we'd almost been intimate.
"You're probably the sacrificial lamb," she said. "The what?" I
said. "The human sacrifice, you know, to the gods, for peace,"
she said. "I figure it's got to be you, because I recognize all
the rest of them, and they're friends." "You've got to be kidding
me," I said. "No, we all work for peace in our various ways, and
then once a year we get together and have this dinner." "But why
me?" I said. "That's Marguerite's job. She does the research all
year, and she tries to pick someone who won't be missed, someone
who's not giving in a positive way to society, someone who
is essentially selfish. Her choices are very carefully considered
and fair, I think, though I am sorry it's you this time. I think

I could get to like you," she said. I picked at my food. "Well,
I guess I was a rather good choice, except that some people really
like my music. They even say it heals them," I said. "I'm sure
it does," Carmen said, "but Marguerite takes everything into
consideration. She's very thorough."

A More Prosperous Nation

When I went out to weed my garden, I found a wild
baby in it. It snarled at me, and I ran. I had read that
they were becoming a problem in this part of the state. No
one knew where they came from, but they were known to be
incredibly quick and vicious. I went back in the house
and locked the door. Through the kitchen window, I watched
it eat a dozen tomatoes. Then it threw up, and started
eating more. It was a disgusting little creature. The
article I had read advised shooting them on sight "to stop
the epidemic." The creature was eating my flowers by the
fistful. Then it rolled around in the dirt, laughing.
I dialed 911 and reported the wild baby. "Stay in your house.
Do not leave your house," the woman said. Two minutes
later there was a squad car in my driveway. The officers
got out with their shotguns. I didn't want to watch the
slaughter, so I went into the living room and picked up the
paper, but, of course, I couldn't read. I waited tensely
for the explosions. I waited and waited, but there were none.
I went to the kitchen window and looked around. There were
no officers in sight, and no wild baby. I walked around
the house, peering through each window. Nothing, save for
the police car in my driveway with its cherry light still
turning. Of course I had been told not to leave the house
under any circumstances, but this was too much. I didn't own
a gun, so I grabbed a long, sharp kitchen knife. Near the
garden, the grass was stained with blood, and there was
evidence of a tremendous struggle. I was shaking as I
prowled around the house. I figured the baby had eaten the

two policemen and would now be quite huge, but perhaps it would be sleepy, too, after such a giant meal. It couldn't still be hungry, or was I kidding myself? I finished circling the house without incident. The officers were sitting on my door stoop having a smoke. "I thought that thing had eaten both of you," I said. "Nice place you've got here," one of them said. "That wasn't a real wild baby," the other one said. "That was just a baby someone didn't want. They're a dime a dozen. Most of them learn to get by on their own, but, of course, some don't make it." "What about the blood in the yard?" I said. "It took a bite out of my ankle, nothing serious," he said. "And where did it go?" I asked. "It was too fast. We didn't see where it went. It will probably be back, but it's nothing to worry about," he said. "But it's my home," I said. "I need to feel safe, my garden." "Share the bounty," the first officer said. "You've got plenty to go around. They're only babies, you know."

Mr. Twiggy

Fatty told Smiley that Slim was getting
on his nerves. Slim told Smiley to mind his
own business. Smiley said, "This is my business,
because you and Fatty are my two best friends."
Red said, "What about me, Smiley, aren't I one
of your best friends, too?" "Of course you are,
Red. I'm just trying to patch things up between
Slim and Fatty. Friends like them shouldn't
be fighting," Smiley said. "I'm not fighting
with Fatty. He's fighting with me," Slim said.
"You called me Fatty the fatty," Fatty said.
"Well, if you can't take a joke, it's not my
fault," Slim smirked. "Come on, boys," Smiley
said, "can't you hear yourselves bickering like
a couple of old maids. Why don't you shake hands
and make up and stop all this name-calling."
"Can I shake hands, too?" Red said. "I don't
want to shake hands with Red," Fatty said. Slim
said, "Red once called me a beanpole." "I did
not," Red said. "I said you resembled a bean-
pole." "You boys are making my smile droop,"
Smiley said. "See what we've gone and done,"
Fatty said. "It's a bad day when Smiley's
smile droops," Slim added. "I never even had
a smile," Red sighed. "Let's make up, Slim,"
Fatty proposed. "Oh, alright," Slim said,
shaking Fatty's hand. "Warriors in the pursuit
of the higher truths, always searching, seeking,

embracing, never shirking, for the soul is
fashioned by love and we are ever marching
toward it," Smiley said. "Wow," Red said.
"Amazing," Fatty said. "Are you alright,
Smiley?" Slim inquired. "A tad . . . wan," he said,
and then his legs buckled, and he collapsed.
Red ran around in circles, squeaking. "He'll
be alright," Fatty said. "He's just resting
for the long march." "Marching hurts my feet,"
Slim said. "I'm not going on any long march.
And, besides, Smiley wasn't in his right mind
when he made that speech." "Mr. Know-it-all,"
Fatty said, "Mrs. Lazy, Mr. Too-good-to-march.
Mr. Twiggy."

Bounden Duty

I got a call from the White House, from the
President himself, asking me if I'd do him a personal
favor. I like the President, so I said, "Sure, Mr.
President, anything you like." He said, "Just act
like nothing's going on. Act normal. That would
mean the world to me. Can you do that, Leon?" "Why,
sure, Mr. President, you've got it. Normal, that's
how I'm going to act. I won't let on, even if I'm
tortured," I said, immediately regretting that "tortured"
bit. He thanked me several times and hung up. I was
dying to tell someone that the President himself called
me, but I knew I couldn't. The sudden pressure to
act normal was killing me. And what was going on
anyway. I didn't know anything was going on. I saw
the President on TV yesterday. He was shaking
hands with a farmer. What if it wasn't really a
farmer? I needed to buy some milk, but suddenly
I was afraid to go out. I checked what I had on.
I looked "normal" to me, but maybe I looked more
like I was trying to be normal. That's pretty
suspicious. I opened the door and looked around.
What was going on? There was a car parked in front
of my car that I had never seen before, a car that
was trying to look normal, but I wasn't fooled.
If you need milk, you have to get milk, otherwise
people will think something's going on. I got into
my car and sped down the road. I could feel those
little radar guns popping behind every tree and bush,

but, apparently, they were under orders not to stop me. I ran into Kirsten in the store. "Hey, what's going on, Leon?" she said. She had a very nice smile. I hated to lie to her. "Nothing's going on. Just getting milk for my cat," I said. "I didn't know you had a cat," she said. "I meant to say coffee. You're right, I don't have a cat. Sometimes I refer to my coffee as my cat. It's just a private joke. Sorry," I said. "Are you alright?" she asked. "Nothing's going on, Kirsten. I promise you. Everything is normal. The President shook hands with a farmer, a real farmer. Is that such a big deal?" I said. "I saw that," she said, "and that man was definitely not a farmer." "Yeah, I know," I said, feeling better.

Shiloh

On Monday, Miss Francis told her sixth-grade
class that she was getting married soon. The class
was very happy for her, and they asked her lots of
questions about her wedding plans. They never once
mentioned the Civil War. On Tuesday, she came in
late wiping tears from her eyes, and told them
there was going to be no wedding. The class let out
a collective sigh. They tried to console her through-
out the hour. No one mentioned Appomattox. On Wed-
nesday, she surprised them all by announcing that the
wedding would, indeed, take place, and that it was
going to be bigger and fancier than originally planned.
The class cheered and applauded. They wanted to know
all the details. She drew a picture of her gown on
the blackboard. She told them all about the food
and the music. Little Rory sat in the back of the
class listening, but what he saw was Pickett's charge
up the ridge at Gettysburg, the mayhem and slaughter,
the horse shot and collapsing, a total of 51,000 dead.
And four months later, Lincoln's great speech at the
cemetery, 267 words, given in four minutes. Rory knew
the speech by heart, and was saying it to himself,
barely able to hold back tears, when Rebecca Crothers
had the impertinency to ask Miss Francis if she was a
virgin. "Long ago and far away," Miss Francis replied.
Rory pictured her camped beside the battlefield,
nervously waiting for her man, who would never return.

I Never Meant to Harm Him

I was sitting at my desk in my second-floor
study when this helicopter pulled right up to the
window. A man was leaning out of it shouting some-
thing at me, but of course I couldn't hear a word.
I went to the window and opened it. It was still
almost impossible to hear anything over the roar of
the engine and the whir of the blades. I kept shouting,
"What? I can't hear you." "Let the boy go!" he said.
"I don't have any boy in here," I said. "Let him go,"
he said. "There's no boy in here," I said. "You've
made some kind of mistake. I don't have any boy," I
shouted. They finally flew away and one of them waved
to me. I went back to work, somewhat rattled. It took
me a while to regain my concentration. I was plotting
my trip down the Amazon, but now when I pictured me
paddling the dugout canoe, I also saw a small boy
nestled in there, sometimes sleeping, other times
pointing out large water snakes near us. The boy
seemed very familiar to me, but, in truth, I knew not
who he was. As the days and nights passed into weeks,
our supplies dwindled. The rainforests were full of
unimaginable sounds, screeches and hollering during
the night that made sleep almost impossible. The boy
was brave, but rarely spoke. He stared at me with his
big, brown eyes. He trusted me with his life, but more
and more I had no idea how we were going to get out
of there, or why we had come. At one point, several
naked Indians stood on the shore with their blowguns

and watched us pass. I wanted to ask for help, but
was afraid for the boy. It was so hot and humid I
was nearly delirious. The boy dozed during the worst
of it. I had no memory of kidnapping him, but where
did he come from? The crocodiles eyed us lazily, but
they're not lazy, they're sly. I've seen them snap up
a tapir or an anteater in a flash. One mistake and
you're lunch. Somewhere there's a rivertown where we
can replenish our supplies, but, as it turns out, the
map is unreliable. Whose boy is this? I never meant
to harm him. He's beautiful but we're drifting. I
have no strength. Surely he can see that. It was our
destiny all along. The sun, the river, and then the night.
And then nothing. "It's okay," he said, "I like being
with you. We're having fun."

Swoon

One of Daniela's breasts fell out of her blouse
during dinner in our favorite restaurant. I liked
looking at it and didn't say anything. The waiter
liked looking at it, too, and just smiled. The other
diners tried not to stare, but some of the men couldn't
help themselves. Daniela takes a certain pride in her
breasts, so perhaps it wasn't an accident. I knew I
should say something to her, but I was also getting
really turned on. It was as if I had never met this
woman before. The public aspect of breast exposure
had a mystery to it that I couldn't name. I said,
"The fileto tre pepe was exceptionally good tonight."
I stared at her breast as if it were about to speak.
"The gnocchi was delicious," it said. "You're looking
especially beautiful tonight," I said. "It's good
to get out and see the people," it said. Daniela
had gone into a swoon or trance of some kind, and the
breast had taken over. When the waiter came for the
bill, he said to Daniela's breast, "Very nice to see you tonight."
The breast blushed, gently swaying in the candlelight.

The Harp

An angel was playing a harp outside of Antonio's
pizzeria. I was already late to meet Walter Culligan,
and he was the man who was going to make me rich within
ten years. Other people had stopped and were listening
to her. They all had these dreamy smiles on their faces.
The angel stroked the harp with her long, white arms as
if she were kneading their souls. She knew how good it
made them feel, and this brought her great pleasure, you
could tell. The music was like nothing I had ever heard
before. It rose and fell and swirled and zigzagged, always
with silence in its heart, and eternity stitched through
every note. I had to ask myself what she was doing here,
but, then, I didn't really need an answer. More and more
people had gathered. The astonishment of sudden joy kept
all lips sealed. The angel's arms were swimming wildly
over the strings. I couldn't think. I couldn't even
remember my own name, but I was happy, if that was the
right word, in a way I had never been before. Of course,
I was in love with her. I would have given anything to
be alone with her, just to hear her speak. The crowd had
spilled out into the street and was blocking traffic. A
mounted policeman rode up and was studying the situation,
but it seems he, too, was quickly entranced. Everyone
was in love with her—women, children, old men and young.
"She's mine," I shouted. "The hell she is, she's mine,"
someone yelled. And that's when the brawl broke out. I
started swinging at anyone within range. And I was getting
pounded left and right and from behind. The policeman

called for help, and started bopping the good citizens of
the town with his nightstick. In the midst of the chaos,
I remembered my name and my appointment with Walter Culligan
and my future wealth. Someone had broken my nose, and I
was bleeding. I was trying to push my way through the
free-for-all, when I saw that the angel had been knocked
to the sidewalk. She was bruised and crying. I knew I
had to save her. With a surge of strength, I threw people
aside, one after another, until, at last, I grabbed her
hand and pulled her up. "This happens every time," she
said. "I guess I really should give it up, but I love
playing that harp. And I love people. The music is meant
to heal them, bring them peace. Look at you, you're
bleeding." She had a deep, gravelly voice, like a barroom
angel, not an angel angel. "Well, maybe it was more peace
than we could stand," I said. The police had dispersed
the crowd by now. The harp stood by itself undamaged.
"My granddaddy gave me that harp," she said. "Ain't it
beautiful." "It's like a golden ship of light," I said.

The Loon

A loon woke me this morning. It was like waking up
in another world. I had no idea what was expected of me.
I waited for instructions. Someone called and asked me
if I wanted a free trip to Florida. I said, "Sure. Can
I go today?" A man in a uniform picked me up in a limousine,
and the next thing I know I'm being chased by an alligator
across a parking lot. A crowd gathers and cheers me on.
Of course, none of this really happened. I'm still sleeping.
I don't want to go to work. I want to know what the loon is
saying. It sounds like ecstasy tinged with unfathomable
terror. One thing is certain: at least they are not speaking
of tax shelters. The phone rings. It's my boss. She says,
"Where are you?" I say, "I don't know. I don't recognize
my surroundings. I think I've been kidnapped. If they make
demands of you, don't give in. That's my professional advice."
Just then, the loon let out a tremendous looping, soaring,
swirling, quadruple whoop. "My god, are you alright?" my
boss said. "In case we do not meet again, I want you to know
that I've always loved you, Agnes," I said. "What?" she said.
"What are you saying?" "Good-bye, my darling. Try to remember me
as your ever loyal servant," I said. "Did you say you loved
me?" she said. I said, "Yes," and hung up. I tried
to go back to sleep, but the idea of being kidnapped had me
quite worked up. I looked in the mirror for signs of torture.
Every time the loon cried, I screamed and contorted my face
in agony. They were going to cut off my head and place it on
a stake. I overheard them talking. They seemed like very
reasonable men, even, one might say, likeable.

Kingdom Come

One night, after dinner, Amy announced to me that she
was pregnant. In our three years of marriage, we had never
even mentioned children, so, in my shock, I had to sort of
fake my response, until I could figure out how I really felt.
"That's so great, Amy," I said. "We're going to be parents.
You've made me the happiest man in the world." "It's kind
of a surprise, though, isn't it? I mean, it wasn't as though we were
trying," she said. "That's probably the best way, when you're
not trying. It proves that it was really meant to be," I said.
In the weeks that followed, I tried to picture us taking care
of a tiny baby. I could see a featherless baby bird, squawking
hideously, and me, crawling toward it with an eyedropper, which,
soon, turned into a dagger. Amy was crouched on top of the
couch like a gargoyle, snarling and hissing. That's about as
far as I got trying to imagine us as parents. We didn't tell
anyone our good news. We didn't even talk about it. If Amy
was seeing a doctor, she didn't mention it to me. We were
sailing through some very unreal territory, and the baby was
the captain of our death ship. I watched baseball on TV all
the time, rooting and shouting like a madman, when, in fact,
I had no idea who was playing or what was going on. It was
just to clutter up the empty space in my life that the baby had
created. Amy sat there with me and, occasionally, shouted
something like "Kill those bastards!" Then, she'd glance at
me, almost coquettishly, and smile, hoping I might be a little
proud of her, which I was. She was swelling up with each passing
week. I thought of her belly as a piñata, and, one day, when
I was properly blindfolded, I would beat on it with a stick,
and out would come wonderful candies and fruits and gifts.

Amy should have worn the head of an elephant, and roared loudly
whenever she turned corners in the house. She was that large.
I began to worship her, and, at the same time, fear her. When-
ever I brought tea and cookies to her, I bowed, and she
accepted this gesture of obeisance without comment, as though
it were her due. She was the Queen, and I, her humble servant.
I took great pride in the performance of my many duties. I did
everything but bathe her. That was an entirely separate operation
jobbed out to independent contractors. I think we both forgot
that a baby had anything to do with any of this. There was so
much to do as it was. I sewed enormous, bejeweled gowns for
the lady. I baked all night. I cooked. I shopped for delicacies.
I chauffeured her to important balls and waited by the side of
the car for hours, counting the stars to keep myself awake.
Not once did I feel sorry for myself, or question my devotion.
And, then, one day she said to me, "Jason, I think it's coming."
"What's coming?" I said. "The baby," she said. My mind went
blank. I literally could not comprehend her words. Our recent
life had been so grand, even though I was a mere servant. "But,
your Czarina," I said, "there is no room in this house for a baby,
and, besides, I have no time. My time is entirely devoted to
satisfying your needs, which, if you will forgive my saying so,
are many. A baby would break this poor camel's back."
"Be that as it may," she said, "the baby is coming." That night,
I was filled with foreboding. I could hear the pounding hooves
of the wild tribes of Genghis Khan coming over the mountains
to rape and pillage our little kingdom, and I cried for mercy,
but there was none. There was only the little baby from now on.

The Radish

I was holding this really exemplary radish in my hand.
I was admiring its shape and size and color. I was imagining
its zesty, biting taste. And when I listened, I even thought
I could hear it singing. It was unlike anything I had ever
heard, perhaps an Oriental woman from a remote mountain village
singing to her rabbit. She's hiding in a cave, and night has
fallen. Her parents had decided to sell her to the evil prince.
And he and his thousand soldiers were searching for her everywhere.
She trembled in the cold and held the rabbit to her cheek. She
whispered the song in a high, thin voice, like a reed swaying
by itself on a bank above a river. The rabbit's large, brown ears
stood straight up, not wanting to miss a word. Then I dropped
the radish into my basket and moved on down the aisle. The store
was exceptionally crowded, due to the upcoming holiday. My cart
jostled with the others. Sometimes it pretended we were in a cock-
fight, a little cut here, some bleeding. Now the advantage is mine.
I jump up and spur the old lady, who's weak and ready to fall.
I spot a mushroom I really want. It's within reach. You could
search all day and never find a mushroom like that. I could smell
it sizzling in butter and garlic. I could taste it garnishing my
steak. Suddenly, my cart is rammed and I'm reeling for my balance.
I can't even see who the enemy is. Then I'm hit again and I'm
sprawling up against the potatoes. I've been separated from my
cart. I look around desperately. "Have you seen my cart?" I ask
a man dressed in lederhosen and an alpine hat. "I myself have
misplaced my mother's ashes. How could I know anything about your
cart," he said. "I'm sorry to hear about your mother," I said.
"Was it sudden, or was it a long, slow, agonizing death, where

you considered killing her yourself just to put her out of her pain?"
"Is that your cart with the radish in it?" he said. "Oh, yes,
thank you, thank you a thousand times over, I can't thank you
enough," I said. "Schmuck," he said. The mushroom of my dreams,
of course, was long gone, and the others looked sickly, like they
were meant to kill you, so I forged on past the kohlrabi and
parsnips. I hesitated at the okra. A flood of fond memories
overcame me. I remembered Tanya and her tiny okra, so firm and
tasty, one Christmas long ago. There was a fire in the fireplace
and candlelight, music, and the crunch, crunch, crunch of the okra.
I have never been able to touch okra since that sacred day.
We were in the Klondike, or so it seemed to me then. Tanya had
a big dog, and it ate the roast, and we had a big laugh, but now
I don't think it's funny. I remember the smell of that roast,
as if it were cooking this very minute, and I can see Tanya
bending over to check on it. How did we ever get out of there
alive? And what happened to Tanya? I look around, peaches and
plums. I'm butted from behind. "Watch it," I say to no one in
particular. Eight eyes are glaring at me. "I'm moving," I say.
But I can't move. The rabbit says, "Tonight we will meet our
death, but it will be beautiful and we will be brave and not
afraid. You will sing to me and I will close my eyes and dream
of a garden where we will play under the starlight, and that's
where the story ends, with me munching a radish and you laughing."
"I can't move," I said.

Return to the City of White Donkeys

Polly tried to tell me that there was an underground
city beneath ours. "The people are very pale, but they can
see in the dark. Of course, there are no cars or anything
like that, but a few have carts pulled by albino donkeys.
They live on root vegetables, potatoes, carrots, radishes
and onions. Oh yes, and grubs, they love grubs. Their houses
are made of mud. They've never seen the sky, or light of
any kind, never seen a sunset, so they don't miss them. They
fall in love, much as we do. They experience joy and pain
and sorrow much the same," she said. "You really believe this,
don't you?" I said. "Oh yes, quite definitely, for you see,
Charles, I was born there and grew up there, and it was only
by accident that I escaped. I was blinded for several months,
and only slowly gained my sight back. 'Escaped' is really the
wrong word, because I never wanted to leave. I wasn't unhappy
in the least. I missed my family terribly," she said. I had
known Polly for years and she had never told me this story.
She was awfully pale, and her eyes were a milky grey-blue, but
an underground city was a bit much to take. She was a very
intelligent woman, an astute observer of politics, which was what
we usually talked about. So I let it pass. I changed the subject,
but Polly remained in a melancholy mood and was mostly silent.
A short time later I said good-bye. I promised to return next
Saturday for our weekly visit. I had tried to remain cool during
Polly's revelation, but once I had left I became deeply disturbed.
Either she was a complete lunatic, which she had successfully
disguised all these years, or she was having a sudden nervous

breakdown, or there was this city beneath ours with all these
pale people sitting down to a dinner of grub worms and radishes
in utter darkness. I couldn't get these thoughts off my mind
all week. There were times I wanted to believe her, even offer
to help her find a way back home. And other times when I just
worried about her sanity and well-being, and what, if anything,
I could do to help her. Saturday came, and I felt apprehensive
about the visit. I bought her a box of chocolates. She was seated
in the dark, and seemed particularly solemn. After a while, she
said, "My mother is dying. I must go home and be with her."
"I'm sorry," I said. I didn't question how she knew. "As you
might guess, there are certain logistical problems. I have only
the faintest memory of where I surfaced all those years ago.
I was only a child at the time, and the shock of the light
is all that has stayed with me," she said. "You must try to
remember, anything, a church steeple, a farmhouse, a road, any-
thing," I said. She put her hands over her eyes and tried to
recapture when she emerged from the earth as a child. "I was
completely blinded, by the light," she said. "You must see
something," I said. "I can't," she said. "Wait. Yes, there is
a church steeple, I can see it now, it's fuzzy, it's a blur,
but it is definitely a church steeple, maybe fifty yards away,"
she said. And, so, we drove around. There were only seven
steeples in the area. Polly was excited, and I was, too. At
each church, Polly got out of the car and wandered around in
fields, and sometimes people's yards. She looked like a dream
out there, the wind plowing through her hair and lifting her

white dress. She looked so happy. Then, when she had finally
given up on the seventh, she started walking back to the car
and something happened. It was late afternoon and the sun was
in my eyes, so I didn't actually see it happen. All I know is,
I never saw Polly again.

The Nameless Ones

The moths come and eat everything within sight. They
come by the millions and darken the sky. You can hear their
jaws munching at night. It's an awful sound, and, in the morning,
the trees are bare, not a leaf anywhere. I closed the windows
and locked the doors, but still they get in. What they are
looking for, I don't know, a potted geranium. They're ravenous.
They won't leave until they are sure there is nothing left.
"There's nothing left," I tell them. And then they're gone.
They rev their engines, the sky darkens for a few moments,
and they're gone. The trees are bare, some of them will never
come back, but it's a bright day. I knocked on Connie's door.
"You can come out now, honey. They're all gone," I said. "Are
you sure?" she said. "I'm sure. Come on out and see for yourself,"
I said. She opened the door. She had one crawling in her hair,
but I didn't want to say anything. "My god, they ate everything.
I could hear them all night long. It was horrible," she said.
"I'm sure they must have gotten into the house." "Well, I've
found a few I've taken care of," I said. "There shouldn't
be any more." Connie slowly poked about the house, investigating.
She found several in each cupboard, which I quickly disposed of,
but not before she could scream. "What the hell are they, anyway?"
she said. "That's the problem. Scientists have never seen any-
thing quite like them before. They don't know what they are.
They don't seem to be related to anything. They're as much in
the dark as we are," I said. "That's just great," she said. "Well,
at least they don't eat livestock and pets." "That's not exactly
true," I said. "What do you mean?" she said. "Well, there have
been some unconfirmed reports of missing cattle and sheep and

a few pets. And one child is missing, but you know how these things are, a certain amount of hysteria has to be taken into account. It will all probably work out," I said. "Whoever heard of a flesh-eating moth?" she said. "It gives me the creeps to even think about it." "Until it's confirmed it's probably best to put it out of your mind," I said. "You know, I hate to admit it, but they were kind of beautiful. They were jet-black with those bright yellow spots on their wings. I almost wish we had kept a couple to remember them by, you know, as pets in jars or something," she said. I was shocked, at first, to hear her say this, but the more I thought about it, the more I agreed that it wouldn't be such a bad thing to have a couple of them around, in captivity, as pets. I reached up and grabbed the one out of her hair. "Ouch," I said, "it bit me." "Put it in something quickly," she said. It continued to gnaw on my hand, but I found a preserve jar and succeeded in getting it in there. My hand was bleeding. I found a clean cloth and wrapped it around it. "Are you alright?" she said. "Yes, but it was going to eat my hand, that's for sure," I said. "Let's see if we can find another one," she said. I suggested we wear gloves this time, and Connie agreed. We pulled out drawers and looked in closets and under the bed with no success. "There's got to be another one somewhere," she said. But there wasn't. Connie finally gave up. She sat staring at the moth in the jar all evening. "No one knows who you are," she said, "and now I've got you. How does it feel to be so alone, to be so beautiful, and have nothing?"

Macaroni

Tamara had gone to visit her sister for a few days and I
was on my own. I was cooking some macaroni and cheese and some
hot dogs when Jacob called. He wanted me to go to a lecture with
him by a novelist called Alexis Volborth, who had just published
a best seller called *War Is Good*. Jacob said it was a very funny
book. I thanked him for the invitation, but said that I had other
plans. Jacob sounded disappointed. I had nearly burnt the macaroni,
but still the dinner was delicious. I savored every bite. I had
even lit candles for the occasion. I had put on some favorite music.
Just as I was finishing up, the phone rang. It was a man calling
himself Wolfgang von Hagen. "Excuse me for bothering you, Mr. Metcalf,
but I heard that you were considering going to the lecture by Alexis
Volborth tonight. I thought you should know that Alexis Volborth is a
traitor of the worst sort, disloyal to his country and single-handedly
responsible for my brother's death. I advise you to stay away from
this most disgraced, most dishonorable of human beings," he said.
"Well, actually, I wasn't planning to go at all, but thanks for the
information," I said. I felt a little edgy as I washed my few dishes.
Why would he call me of all people? When I finished, I went into
the living room and picked up the paper. Another small child had
fallen down a well. Another dog had rescued someone from the flooding
river. The mayor said he had his hands tied. There was nothing he
could do. I put the paper down. The wind was blowing outside.
Branches were scraping the windows. Just then, the phone rang. I
was almost expecting the call. It was Alexis Volborth. He said
Wolfgang von Hagen was a liar, a thief and a murderer. "Do not believe
a word he has said about me. They are all lies, and, worse, if he

gets near you he will mutilate you beyond recognition. Trust me,
I know of what I speak. It is a pity you are not coming to my lecture,
because I would have made you laugh deeply to the bottom of your soul,"
he said. "Nevertheless, it is an honor to speak with you, sir," I
said, hoping to stay on his good side, at least. I lit my pipe
and took a couple of puffs. I must admit, I felt ever so slightly
important, caught in the crossfire, as they say. Without even
leaving my house, my opinions seemed to matter in this international
affair. But what did I really think? I guess I was inclined to
believe both of them. They had no reason to lie to me, a complete
stranger. I lit my pipe and picked up the paper. The phone rang.
It was Jacob. He said, "I'm calling you from the lecture hall. Can
you come and pick me up right now. Something's gone terribly wrong.
Alexis Volborth has been killed. And there are others, I don't know how
many. It's mayhem down here. There are police everywhere."
"I'll be right there," I said. "But, Jacob, stay away from a man
named Wolfgang." "Wolfgang's my only friend," he said.

The Coolest Thing

A long-haired man wearing only a loincloth came dragging
a heavy cross right down the middle of Main Street. People on
both sides of the street stopped and stared. They were speechless
at first, but then, stranger to stranger, they began to share
their outrage. "That's a sacrilege," one of them said, and,
"It's just plain tacky if you ask me." The man carrying the cross
seemed to be really suffering. His bare feet and his hands were
bleeding. The cross must have weighed over a hundred pounds.
He was stooped and breathing heavily. "Take your bloody cross
and go home. You should be ashamed of yourself," someone yelled.
"We should just ignore him," an old woman said. "Where are the
police when you need them," a man with a red tie said. A boy of
ten ran out into the street and shoved the man from behind. He fell
forward and the cross pinned him to the ground. "That wasn't very
nice," someone muttered. The man lay there for a minute, and then
started squirming his way back up. He struggled with the cross
for a few minutes and finally got it back on his shoulder and started
inching forward. "Well, he can't very well nail himself to that cross,"
a man in a panama hat said. "Maybe he's got a friend," a pretty
young woman said. "What's he trying to prove, anyway?" an old man
said. "He thinks he's the only righteous one, and the rest of us
are sinners," a woman holding a poodle said. The dog barked disapproval
of the spectacle. "Well, this is more than I can take," said an
old woman, and huffed away. The crowd was slowly dispersing. The
man with the cross had almost reached the center of town. Some kids
were throwing small stones at him. Mostly they missed. His knees
were bent, and he looked as if he might just regret this whole bright
idea of his. And if he had a friend, now would be a good time for

him to appear. But no one did appear. Even the kids were running down the street away from him, chasing one another and screaming something. A police car pulled up. The officer leaned out the window and said, "You'll have to get that thing out of here. It's obstructing traffic." "I'm trying to move it as fast as I can," the bleeding man said. "Well, I'll have to arrest you if you're not gone from here by the time I get back," he said, and sped off. The man dragged the cross to the side of the road and put it down. He sat down on the curb and buried his face in his hands. The cross started to smoke, slowly at first. Then, suddenly, it burst into flames. The man opened his eyes and jumped up, quivering. The cross was blazing. He backed up onto the lawn of the new bank and watched it in awe as it was quickly consuming itself. The kids returned and said, "Is that the coolest thing you've ever seen, or what?" Motorists stopped to admire. The man with the panama hat came by and said, "It's like a work of art. It's a statement on our times. Of course I don't know what that statement is, but I'm sure it has some sort of meaning." The woman with the poodle said, "It's so beautiful I think I'm going to cry." "I carry a clean handkerchief for just such occasions," the man said, offering it to her. "Why, thank you," she said, dabbing her eyes. Several blocks away, one could hear the siren of the fire truck just starting up, but it was almost too late as there were only the traces of smoldering ash left by the side of the road. The man and the woman had walked away together conversing on some topic of mutual concern.

THE GHOST
SOLDIERS

The Native Americans

"We found them on your lawn this morning, about seventy-
five of them," the officer said. "What are they?" I said. "Well,
they're some kind of Native Americans, we don't know what kind yet,
but we will. We used an electrical device to paralyze them, but
they'll start coming to in about twenty-four hours. Some of them
will only live for about an hour, and others could live as long
as sixty years. So we'll start in reeducating them right away,"
he said. "But where did they come from?" I said. "Well, we don't
really know, but some of our scientists think they just rose up
out of the ground, some signal goes off in them, like a timer,"
he said. "You mean all this time I have been living in a cemetery?"
I said. "Apparently," he said. "Well, that explains a lot," I
said. "What do you mean?" he said. "Just recently I have felt
the house shake a lot at night, and I thought I heard distant
cries, and I would wake covered in sweat, which I thought was blood,"
I said. "Why don't you come down here tomorrow morning and we'll
show you some of the men," he said. "Thank you, Officer," I said.
Of course I was made miserable by the thought that these men had
been buried beneath my lawn all these years, but what could I do?
The lawn was an unholy mess. It would have to be completely redone
in the spring. I showed up at the police department around 10:00
the next morning as told. There behind glass doors were these
half-awake men, moaning and shuffling about. "They don't look very
dangerous," I said to the officer. "That's why I wanted you to come
in early. I didn't want you to see that part of it," he said.

"What do you do then?" I said. "More electricity. Then slowly we start to reeducate. Some of them will go quite far," he said. "And what about the others?" I said. "Oh, we'll rebury them with a jolt that will keep them down a good long time," he said. "In my yard?" I said. "That's their native ground," he said.

Abducted

Mavis claimed to have been abducted by aliens. Maybe she was, I don't know. She said they had intercourse with her, but it was different. They placed a finger in the middle of her forehead and made a buzzing sound. She said it felt better than the other kind of intercourse. I asked her if I could try it and she said no. Not long after that Mavis disappeared for good. She didn't say good-bye to anyone and no one knew where she went. I started dreaming about her. Frequently, they were disturbing dreams, but the ones that involved aliens were very soothing. I think I secretly longed to be abducted. Of course I never confessed this to anyone. I'm not saying I believed Mavis, but I do believe she experienced what she said she did. People see things that aren't there all the time. Some of those people are crazy and some aren't. Mavis wasn't crazy. She wasn't my lover, but we were good friends and I missed her. But life went on. I had a couple of beers with Jared once or twice a week. I went out to dinner or to a movie with Trisha occasionally. Once I knocked on the door of Mavis's old apartment and a woman who spoke no English answered. There was an article in the paper about a woman who had been found at the bottom of a lake. Police had not been able to identify her. I went down to the morgue right away. "I'd like to see the body of the woman who drowned in the lake," I said. "I'm sorry. That's not possible," the man said. "But she may be a friend of mine," I said. "The police have given me strict orders. No one is to see her," he said. "But I could possibly identify her," I said. "Trust me, no one could identify what we have here," he said. I left and returned home. Jared came over that night. I told him that I was worried that the woman in the morgue could be Mavis. He said, "Who's Mavis?" I said, "You know damned well who Mavis is. You had several dates with her. I think you might have even been falling in love with her, but she dumped you." "I don't know any Mavis, and I certainly never dated her. My memory's not that bad," he said. "I saw you at Donatello's one night with her," I said. "I've never been to Donatello's," he said. "Jared, why are you doing this?" I said. "I'm just telling you the truth. I've never known a woman named Mavis," he said. Later, after Jared left, I started thinking about it. I couldn't even picture Mavis's face anymore. It was sad. She was being erased. I wanted to put my finger on her forehead, but there was nothing there.

The Ghost Soldiers

I saw a duck fly into a tree today. Boy, you don't see
that very often. It must have been daydreaming. I was out driving
around, and now that I think of it, it had looked over at me just before
impact. It must have felt so stupid. Anyway, I didn't stop to
see how it was. I wanted to, but I was afraid I would embarrass it.
Just that little glance at me may have done it in. I feel lousy about
it, but it really wasn't my fault. I was on my way to the Memorial
Day parade. Suddenly I wanted to see all these veterans in their
uniforms marching down Main Street. But this duck had flown by
and looked at me, and now its body lay crumpled in a heap. I drove on,
not looking back. The police had cordoned off Main Street, so I had to
turn down a side street and look for a parking place. There were no
parking places for blocks, but eventually I found one. There was a
steady stream of people on the sidewalks, all heading for the parade.
I fell in stride beside them. "It's a nice day for a parade," I said
to one little old lady walking beside me. "You think I'm going to fall
for a tired old line like that? You better think again, mister," she
said. "I was just commenting on the weather," I said. "I didn't mean
to offend you." I kept to myself after that. The parade itself was
rather modest. I counted about thirty-five veterans, ranging in age
from eighty-five to eighteen. Several were in wheelchairs, several
more on crutches, two drummers and one horn player. The crowd just
stared at them in silence. Police patrolled the streets as if the
Queen were passing. I looked but saw no Queen. The man beside me
looked at me and said, "The parade's so small because everyone from
this town is always killed. They're just not fit to fight. I don't
know why that is. It must be something in the water. They just refuse
to shoot. It's odd, isn't it. They've done many studies on it, and

they still don't know why it is like that." "Are you trying to pick me up, because, if you are, you're going to have to come up with a better line than that," I said. "What the hell are you talking about?" he said. "I came here to see the Queen, but apparently there's no Queen," I said. "We got rid of all that royalty crap hundreds of years ago," he said. "Oh," I said, "well, nobody told me." I turned and fought my way through the crowd and walked back to my car. The drive home was uneventful, except that I kept imagining this duck flying beside my car looking at me. It was distracting me, as I was not keeping my eye on the road. One minute it was a soulful, almost loving gaze, and the next it felt accusatory. I narrowly missed an oncoming truck, and the driver honked angrily at me. With that, I bade the duck good-bye and concentrated on driving. It's true, almost no one from this town ever came back from any war. They call them the ghost soldiers, much beloved even by their enemies, and I guess that's why I went to the parade, just to feel them march past, that little rush of cold air.

Cricket Cricket

When I am alone on a summer night, and
there is a cricket in the house, I always feel
that things could be worse. Maybe it is raining,
and then thunder and lightning are shaking the
house. The power goes out, and I must grope
around in the darkness for a candle. At last,
the candle is found, but where are the matches?
I always keep them in that drawer. I knock over
a vase, but it doesn't break. Afraid of what
I might break, I return to my chair and sit
there in the darkness. The lightning is striking
all around the house. Then I remember the cricket,
and I listen for its chirping. Soon, the storm
passes, and the lights come back on. An eerie
green silence fills my home. I am worried that
the cricket may have been struck by some light-
ning of its own.

Father's Day

My daughter has lived overseas for a number
of years now. She married into royalty, and they
won't let her communicate with any of her family or
friends. She lives on birdseed and a few sips
of water. She dreams of me constantly. Her husband,
the Prince, whips her when he catches her dreaming.
Fierce guard dogs won't let her out of their sight.
I hired a detective, but he was killed trying to
rescue her. I have written hundreds of letters
to the State Department. They have written back
saying that they are aware of the situation. I
never saw her dance. I was always away at some
convention. I never saw her sing. I was always
working late. I called her My Princess, to make
up for my shortcomings, and she never forgave me.
Birdseed was her middle name.

Waylon's Woman

Loretta had a rooster that was so fierce
nobody could visit her anymore. Loretta loved
that rooster, and the rooster loved Loretta,
thought she was his wife. So the only time
we got to see Loretta was when she came to town.
We'd meet her at Mike's Westview Café and drink
beer with her all night. The rooster's name
was Waylon, and she'd talk about Waylon all
night, and if you didn't know better you'd think
she was talking about her husband. Well, I knew
better, and I still thought she was talking about
her husband. "Waylon wasn't feeling very good
this morning." "Waylon was real sweet to me
last night." "Waylon is so handsome, sometimes
I just can't take my eyes off him." She's still
fun to be with, and she seems completely normal
to me. At closing time, we say our good-byes,
and I kiss Loretta, just a little peck, because
I know she is married to a chicken, and I respect
that. Waylon has made her happy in ways I never
could. The starry sky, the police hiding in the
bushes, God, it's good to be alive, I think, and
pee behind my car in the darkness of my own private
darkness.

My Cattle Ranch

I don't remember much about that particular
evening. Jacqueline insisted on showing me her
navel. She claimed that if I touched it, it
would bring me good luck. I have no idea if I
touched it. Dabney was bragging about his winnings
at the horse track. He said he won nine out of
ten races the week before. I told him I didn't
believe him, and he invited me to go to the track
with him. I told him I wasn't a gambling man,
which was a lie. Beatrice came over and showed
me her navel. It seemed to have a little face
in it, which made me laugh. I asked her if I
could touch it, and she said, "Of course, darling."
I didn't want to stop touching it, but after a
while she needed to go to the ladies' room. Adam
told me about his recent surgery. He showed me
his scar and I dropped my drink. Isabel tried to
sell me some cattle. "Isabel," I said, "I'm
not that kind of a man." She lifted her blouse
a little and pointed to her navel. I don't
remember much after that. Some vegetables were
served. Some pottery was broken. Otto Guttchen
showed me a fossil.

Uneasy About the Sounds of Some Night-Wandering Animal

On the way to work this morning, the newsman on the
radio said, "A big part of reality has been removed, it has
been reported. Details are not available at this time. It's
just that, I am told, you will find things different on your
drive to work this morning. Some roads will be missing, whole
areas of the city may be gone. However, the good news is, no
signs of violence have been detected." I turned the radio off.
There wasn't the usual rush hour traffic, for which I was grate-
ful. I wasn't even sure I was on the right road. There were
empty fields where I had remembered rows and rows of apartment
buildings. Then I went into a long tunnel, and I had no memory
of there being a tunnel. When I came out of it, there was nothing,
or, rather, I guess it was a desert, as I had never been in the
desert before. I looked around for signs of the city. A jack-
rabbit scurried across the road, and up ahead a policeman was
leaning against his motorcycle. I slowed down instinctively,
then pulled over to stop. "Good morning, Officer," I said.
"I seem to have taken a wrong turn. Could you tell me where I
am?" "Not exactly," he said. "This seems to be a new area.
It wasn't here before. We're still trying to identify it.
I suggest you drive with caution, because, well, we have no infor-
mation on it as yet." I noticed that he was about to cry. "Well,
thanks," I said. My stomach was sinking. I was certain to be
late to work. I didn't know what to do. Part of me wanted to
drive on, to see what was out there, and part of me wanted to
turn back, though I wasn't certain of what I would find there.
So I drove on for miles and miles, the sand dunes shifting and

stirring, and the occasional hawk or buzzard circling overhead. Then the road disappeared, and I was forced to stop, and looked behind me, but that road, too, was gone, blown over by sand in a few seconds. I got out of the car, glad that I had some water with me. I looked around, and it was all the same. Nothing made any sense. I tried to call Harvey at the office on my cell phone. I couldn't believe when he answered. "Harvey, it's Carl. I'm out here in this new place. It's all sand, and there are no roads," I said. "We'll come get you," he said. "But I don't know where I am, I mean, I don't know if it exists," I said. "Don't be ridiculous, Carl, of course it exists. Just look around and give me something to go by," he said. "There's nothing here. Oh, there was a tunnel some miles back, and a policeman leaning up against his motorcycle. That's the last thing I saw," I said. "Was it the old Larchmont tunnel?" he said. "I don't know, it could have been. I was lost already," I said. "Okay, I'm going to come get you. Just stay put," he said. I waited and waited. And then I just started walking. I know I wasn't supposed to, but I was restless and hoped I might find a way out. I had lost sight of my car and had no idea where I was. The sun was blinding me and I couldn't think straight. I barely knew who I was. And, then, as if by miracle, I heard Harvey's voice call my name. I looked around and couldn't see him. "Carl, Carl, I'm here," he said. And I still couldn't see him. "We've fallen off. We're in the fallen-off zone," he said. "What? What does that mean?" I said. "We've separated. It may be temporary. It's too soon to tell," he said. "But where are we? We must be in some relation

to something," I said. "I think we're in parallel," he said. "Parallel
to what?" I said. "Parallel to everything that matters," he said.
"Then that's good," I said. I still couldn't see him, and night
was coming on. It was a parallel night, much like the other,
and that was some comfort, cold comfort, as they like to say.

Collect Call from Nepal

I popped myself a beer, and went to sit on the porch
with the newspaper. It was six o'clock in the afternoon
on a Saturday, middle of July, beautiful day. But, then,
the phone was ringing. It was a collect call from Katmandu,
Nepal, from Darcy Symonds. I hadn't seen Darcy in years.
"Yes, I'll take it," I said. "Judson, this is Darcy. Listen,
I'm in a lot of trouble here. There's a revolution going on,
and I need to get out of here. The airports are closed. There's
fighting in the streets. I'm suspected of being a spy and an
informer for the government, but I'm not, Judson, I swear it.
You've got to get me out of here," she said. "Okay, Darcy,
calm down. We'll think of something. How can I get ahold
of you? I need to know where you are," I said. "That's the
trouble, you can't. I'm running for my life. The whole town
is on fire," she said. "Call me again when you know where you
are. Meanwhile, I'll see what I can do," I said. "Judson,
there isn't much time," she said. She hung up. I took a long
pull on my beer and picked up the paper. There was a front-page
story about a two-year-old boy whose dog had saved him from
drowning in the town reservoir. And another about a man who
had found a six-foot boa constrictor in his bed. Police suspected
that its owner will be found. Why would Darcy call me after
all these years? And what was I supposed to do? I tried calling
the State Department in D.C., but they put me on hold and then
switched me over to somebody else, who put me on hold, and so on,
until I finally screamed at an actual human being, "My wife is
trapped in Katmandu. They're going to kill her if you don't help
me get her out of there!" "Calm down, sir. What is your wife's

name?" he said. "Darcy Symonds," I said. "And who is going to kill her?" he said. "The revolutionaries. They think she's a spy and an informer," I said. He asked for my phone number and said he would get back to me as soon as he knew something. I drained my beer and got another one. I looked at the weather forecast for tomorrow: another perfect day. I tried to read the article about the mayoral election, but lost interest. Mr. Giddings trimmed his hedges until the last light was gone. I ate some cheese and crackers and a handful of grapes. I waited up most of the night for Darcy to call back, and also for the man from the State Department. The phone never rang. I got out my atlas and looked up Nepal. I read about it in my encyclopedia. But, still, my imagination failed to picture anything, just screaming and gunfire and fires, and Darcy's frightened face I could see, one among the many, running for cover. It was just another bad movie, and yet, she was my wife, or so I now believed, and it had to end happily, safe but for a few scratches, reunited. I sat there staring at the stars and listening for crickets, feeling emptier than I had ever known. "Who's in charge here?" I said. "A few good men is all we'll need. We'll need some technical support. You, Jones, take out the Himalayas. Martinez, nullify the Buddha."

The Loser

The pressure was on, and I don't perform well under
pressure. "You're the champ," Jenny said. "You always
succeed. Come on, Travis, you can do it." I stared out
the window at the rain. "I'm a loser. I've always been
a loser. Even when I've won, it's felt like losing. When
I was three years old, I was convinced I would never get
anything right. I don't blame anybody. It's just a feeling
that permeates my very soul," I said. "But you can do any-
thing, Travis. I've seen you. You're amazing," Jenny said.
"That's just fooling with people. Sure, I can take a car
apart and put it back together again, but what does that
prove? I can build a house to keep you out of the rain,
but I'm not fooling myself. That's another matter altogether,"
I said. "You're too hard on yourself," Jenny said. "And
what about all those mountains you've climbed? Everyone
says you're the best. And all that money you've made through
good, honest, hard work?" "That's kid's stuff. Believe me,
I'm a loser. I never get anything right," I said.
We'd had this conversation a hundred times before. It annoyed
me to no end, not the stuff that Jenny was saying. She meant
well, and I knew it. But my part. It sounded so ridiculous.
"Why are we even talking about me?" I said. "You started it,"
she said. "I asked you to kiss me, and you sort of fell apart."
"That's funny, I don't remember that at all. I thought you
asked me if I was going to compete in a tennis championship,"
I said. "I don't know anything about a tennis championship,"
Jenny said. "I was just feeling a little warm and cuddly, and
wanted a kiss." "I'd be more than happy to kiss you," I said.

"No, no, the mood's passed. I'm more worried about your soul,
why you feel that you will never get anything right," she said.
"Did I say that? I've always found that when people start
talking about their souls it's best to leave the room," I said.
"Do you want me to leave the room?" Jenny said. "No. Of course
not. I'm not talking about my soul, am I? Or am I?" I said.
"You were earlier, just for a second. I could leave and come
back. Or I could leave and not come back. Whichever
you prefer. It's your soul. Perhaps you'd like to be alone with
it," she said. "I feel like I'm caught in a whirlpool. I'm
dizzy and I'm sinking. Isn't there anything we can talk about
other than my soul? After all, it's just a butterfly, it's just
a poof," I said. Jenny walked into the kitchen and started
banging some pots and pans around. I shook my head and stood up.
Something was terribly wrong. An egg was hatching in my hand,
the egg of an otter. Otters don't lay eggs, but I was starving.

Map of the Lost World

Things were getting to me, things of no
consequence in themselves, but, taken together,
they were undermining my ability to cope. I needed
a hammer to nail something up, but my hammer wasn't
in the toolbox. It wasn't anywhere to be found.
I broke a dish while putting away the dishes, but
where's the broom? Not in the broom closet. How do
you lose a broom? Where was it hiding? And, then,
later, while making the bed, I found the hammer.
Perhaps it was used as a sleeping-aid device. Then
Kelly called and said she had lost her ring last night
and would I please look under the bed. I looked and
found the broom there. So I decided to sweep under
there to see if I could find her ring. I swept out
a rosary, a spark plug, a snakeskin—three feet long—
a copy of *Robert's Rules of Order,* a swizzle stick,
a jawbreaker, and much more. But no ring. I put the
broom into the broom closet, and started to feel a little
better. I hung the picture and put the hammer into
the toolbox. I made myself a cup of tea, and sat down
in the living room. I had no idea how any of that
stuff could have gotten under my bed. None of it
belonged to me. It was quite a disturbing assortment.
Then I thought of Kelly's ring, and how it could have
fallen behind one of the cushions on the couch. I
drank some tea to calm my nerves. The stuff under
the bed could be the residue of dreams. I drank some
more tea. Then I lifted the first cushion. There

was about three dollars' worth of change and a monkey
carved out of teak. I didn't like the monkey at all,
but I was happy to have the three dollars. Under the
next cushion there was a small glass hand, a lead soldier
in a gas mask, a key ring with three keys, and a map of
Frankfurt, Germany. I sipped my tea. My hands were
shaking. The whole morning was frittering away with
nonsense. I had work to do, or, if not that, then I
should be relaxing. I wasn't going to look for Kelly's ring
anymore at all. I sat there without moving, my mind
drifting over the clouds. I was pulling a yak over
a mountaintop, hauling water and rice to a dead wise man,
who knows nothing, says nothing.

How I Met Mary

It wasn't for everyone. God knows, there was little enough
to go around. I had to fight for my little bit. It got pretty
rough in there. Whoever planned the thing had their head in a
bucket. Before long mayhem broke out. I tried to leave but some-
body kept dragging me back and throwing me on the floor. That's
when I first saw Mary. Of course, I didn't know her name then,
but she was struggling to get up and had a tear in her blouse. I
wanted to help her, but I was in no position. Some three-hundred-
pound lug was sitting on me. I was pounding his chest and screaming.
He didn't care. Hell, he didn't even notice. I saw some guy go
flying through the air, and I realized it was Matthew Quinn, the
organizer. That's when I went unconscious for a few minutes, perhaps
the guy had hit me, I wasn't sure. When I woke, he was no longer
sitting on me, so I tried to stand. I saw this woman, Mary, hiding
under a table, and I started to crawl toward her. Somebody fell
on my back and flattened me. I lay there, trying to breathe. Some-
body bent down and said, "Would you care for a weenie in a blanket?"
"I'd love one, thanks," I said. I choked it down, then tried rolling
the man on my back off me. "Which candidate are you for?" he said.
"I'm still trying to make up my mind," I said. I crawled forward a
little more. A pitcher of lemonade crashed in front of me, splinters
of glass everywhere. So I stood up. Matthew Quinn was standing in
front of me. "I'm so glad you could come. A really good-spirited
discussion is just what we need right now," he said. "Don't you
think it's gone a little too far," I said. "It's important to know
what the other guy is thinking so we can come to a consensus and rally
around the cause," he said. Just then something buckled my knees
and I was on the ground again amid all the broken glass. My hands

and knees were bleeding, but I crawled on toward Mary. Matthew was knocked backwards and I stopped to see how he was. "My nose is broken. It's nothing. It's happened many times before," he said. "I think we're getting close to a consensus," I said. "See, what did I tell you. It just takes time," he said, bleeding profusely. I was getting close to Mary. I reached out my hand toward her. She found a steak knife on the floor and aimed it toward me. "Don't come any closer or I'll kill you, I swear it," she said. "I wanted to help you," I said. "You're an animal, just like the rest of them," she said. "No, I swear, I had no idea this was going to turn out like this. I thought it would be a good idea to discuss the issues," I said. She faked a jab at me and then said, "Yeah, me too, but I don't think I'm willing to die for them." "My name's Glenn," I said. "I'm Mary," she said. "Do you think we could find a way out of here?" I said. "We'd probably be killed or at least maimed," she said. "Most of the action is in the center of the room right now. Why don't we crawl close to the walls until we can reach that door," I said. We crawled over Eric McKenna, who was out cold. Peter Furman smashed into the wall behind us. I saw Scott Guest fly through the window. And finally we were able to slip out the door. "Those people are crazy," she said. "They're just concerned citizens," I said. That made her laugh. "What were they supposed to be talking about?" she said. "Oh, you know, the usual stuff, faulty mucilage, cross-eyed frogs, obscure birdsongs," I said. "I never heard any of those things mentioned," she said. "They were just warming up to them," I said. "Well, at least they really care about something," she said. "Those are the caringest people you'll ever meet," I said.

Long Live the Queen

When the little man opened his mouth he squawked like a
bird. So I grabbed him by the shoulders, spun him around and
threw him down the steps. I ran down the steps and picked him
up. He had a bump on his forehead, but, other than that, he seemed
to be in fine shape. "What do you say now?" I said. "Was it
that bit about the Queen that ticked you off?" he said. I socked
him in the eye. Then I socked him in the other eye. He squawked
and fell to the ground. I picked up his feet and dragged him
across the floor. "Stand up," I said. His legs thrashed around
a bit, but finally he was able to stand, swaying slightly. "Do
you suppose I could have a glass of water?" he said. "Certainly,"
I said, and fetched him his glass of water. I watched him gulp
it down, and then I said, "See this hammer. I am going to hit
you on the head with it." "That will surely hurt," he said. I
raised the hammer and brought it down on his head. Again, he slumped
to the ground. I made myself a cheese sandwich and ate it in the
other room. When I went back he was still out, so I filled up his
water glass and threw it in his face. He opened his eyes and
looked at me. "Who are you?" he said. "Never mind who I am. Stand
up. You spend far too much time napping. It's not good for you,"
I said. He struggled and fell over several times. Finally, I lent
him a hand and he made it to his feet. I picked the whip off
the chair. "You're going to like this," I said. "Turn around."
I lashed him a good one. He let out a squeak. I lashed him twenty
times all told. Blood soaked through his shirt. "Oh, my," he said,
"you are certainly an expert with that device." "Why, thank you,"
I said, "I do take a certain pride in my technique." He was covered
in sweat and his hair was standing on end. "Perhaps you would

like a little rest before we move on to the next step?" I said. "A little rest would be most welcome," he said. "Have a seat," I said. He was breathing rather heavily. Both his eyes were black. "It has occurred to me, sir," he said. "Of course, the matter of an explanation is strictly voluntary." "I don't owe it to you," I said. "Oh, yes, sir, I understand that," he said. "However, since you've been so cooperative, I will tell you this: it has nothing to do with the Queen," I said. He stared at me with his mouth open. "That's it, that's all you're going to tell me?" he said. "Don't you feel better now?" I said. "Yes, sir. Thank you, sir," he said. "Well, I think we've had enough of a rest. Back to work," I said. I threw him against the wall, then kneed him in the stomach. I threw him back against the wall, then smashed him in the face. When he fell to the floor, I kicked him in the ribs. He lay there moaning and sputtering. I lay down beside him. "You're quite a remarkable man, you know," I said, "with many admirable qualities. The Queen would like to meet you for tea. She's a single lady now that her husband, the King, has died. She's very attractive for her age, which I believe is the same as yours. I don't mean to put any ideas in your head, but I hope you'll think it over," I said. "Over my dead body," he said.

Cleaning Out the Desk

I was working at my desk, straightening papers and throwing
things away. I opened one drawer and there was a paper bag with
a baloney sandwich in it that must have been three years old. I found
some notecards with hieroglyphics carefully written on them. I
also found an envelope containing a clip of someone's hair. It
must have been the hair of someone I loved once, but I couldn't
remember. Then there was a long letter from someone named Seth,
accusing me of stealing his material and making a fortune off of
it and never giving him a dime. First off, I have never made a
fortune from anything, and secondly, I'm not a thief. I don't even
know what kind of material he is referring to. The letter's dated
ten years ago. I tossed it in the trash. I kept digging. There
were photographs of children, distant relatives of mine, but I'd
never met them and didn't know their names. Perhaps they'd visit
me in my old age, not that I wanted them to. And here is a postcard
from Lola. The next day she rode a horse off into the mountains
and was never heard of again. My darling Lola, she had such plans.
There was a small jade Buddha in the back of the drawer. I remember
I carried it for luck for many years. I don't know why it ended
up back there, retired or punished. In another drawer I found
notes on the Oracle of Delphi, "Man, know thyself and be divine,"
and a map of the Delaware River. I seem to remember a plan to go
exploring there. Then a stack of letters from my old friend Beverly
Babcock. She moved to Greece and fell in love with a fisherman.
The letters stopped and mine were returned. She had trained to
be an opera singer and I thought her voice was quite good. I guess
I loved Beverly, but I never told her. Beneath her letters there
was a guide to the subway systems of Antwerp. That would come in

handy if I ever went to Antwerp. There were several old coins in plastic bags. And a postcard from Denise in Hawaii saying they were having a great time, and wishing I was there. There was an antique toy milk truck with half its paint chipped off. I remembered it from my childhood. Why would I save a thing like that? It troubled me to think about it. I shut the drawer and broke for lunch. I made myself a sandwich and sat down at the table. It's funny, I never believed Lola died in the mountains of Arizona. I thought she got herself another identity. I imagined that she had something dark in her past that she was trying to escape. That was just my way of keeping her alive a little longer. And Beverly, I can see her singing in church in that small fishing village on holidays, her man looking on proudly. I wonder if she ever thinks of me. I got up and washed my plate. That little milkman was a terrible driver, always crashing into walls and falling off of tables. We were poor and it was all I had to amuse myself. Poor milkman, such a lousy driver, but he's followed me all these years. The President is missing, I thought. "Oh no," said the Secretary of State, the President has a very busy schedule and he has been temporarily misplaced. We will find him, I assure you." "But he's missing," I said.

National Security

I said, "I want to go home." "I told you, we have no home,"
Anne said. "What happened to our home?" I said. "The government
took it," she said. "What for?" I said. "They said it was for
strategic reasons," she said. And, thus, we commenced our roaming.
Mostly we stayed at campsites along the way. We had a tent and
sleeping bags, a couple of pots and pans. I was confused about what
had happened to us, but I also liked the adventure. Once a man
came over and said that he and his wife would like to share their
dinner with us. Anne said her husband wasn't feeling well. I said,
"I feel great." We sat around their campfire and talked. The man
said he used to be a dentist, but now he was a gold miner. "You
should've been taking those little gold caps out of people's
mouths all along. You'd be rich now," I said. Anne plowed
her elbow into my ribs. "We're heading for the Klondike," his
wife said. "It's best to stay out of the strategic zones," Anne
said. They nodded in unison. "But I still don't know where they
are," I said. They all looked at me, but didn't say anything.
We ate some awful, strange meat and some baked beans, at least I
think that's what they were. Later that night I was sick. In the
morning when we had been on the road about three hours a band of
Indians came riding toward us. "What are we supposed to do?" I
said to Anne. "They've risen up all over the country. They're
on the warpath. They're going to take over the government," she
said. "But what about us right now?" I said. "Just be nice,"
she said. When they came alongside of the car, Anne stopped
and rolled down her window. "Howdy, fellow Americans," she said.
"Can you tell us how to get to Topeka?" he said. "Sure, that's
easy," she said, and proceeded to give him directions. "That's

most helpful," he said. "Have a good day." We drove on into the glaring sun. "Where are we going?" I said. "Do I look like I know where we're going? I just want to get away as far as we can," she said. "What about our old friends?" I said. "You'll just have to make new ones," she said. "Patagonia, is that where we're going?" I said. "No, we're not going to Patagonia. I don't know where we're going," she said. "We're getting low on gas and I don't think there's going to be a station for a long time," I said. "Then we'll have to walk," she said. I was beginning to see how crazed she was and it frightened me. "We don't have anything to eat," I said. "You can kill a jackrabbit," she said. There was an old shepherd up ahead moving his flock across the road. When we pulled to a stop, she said, "Get out and grab one of those sheep and throw it in the backseat." I said, "I'm not going to do that. There's no way." She looked at me, then opened her door, and went and grabbed a sheep around its waist and tried to heft it up. She dropped it and tried again. It took all her strength to drag it over to the car. She finally managed to stuff it in the backseat before the shepherd saw what she had done. He pounded on her window and hit it with his staff. "A curse on you. I put a curse on you!" he shouted. She rolled down her window and yelled back at him, "National Security. It's for your own good."

How to Be a Member

I didn't understand what was expected of me. Maxwell told
me to walk around with an orchid in my hand and then I would be
counted. I did this and then this woman came out and said, "Where's
your teddy bear?" "I was told to bring an orchid," I said. "Orchids
come much later. Right now it is only a teddy bear that counts,"
she said. I started to leave, feeling slightly annoyed. Maxwell
spotted me and came running up. "What are you doing with an orchid?"
he said. "You told me," I said. "Not now, for god's sake. This is
the teddy bear stroll," he said. "I know, I know. I don't know
if I'm up to this thing," I said. "You don't have any choice. It's
required," he said. When I came back clutching my teddy bear,
people were standing around in pairs taking turns slapping one
another. There were no teddy bears in sight. The couples didn't
speak. There were significant pauses between slaps. A man walked
up to me and said, "Where's your partner? Why aren't you slapping?"
I said, "I don't have a partner." "Of course you have a partner.
Everybody has a partner," he said. "I was out getting my teddy
bear," I said. "Teddy bears have got nothing to do with it. This is
the slapping time," he said. I looked around everywhere. There
was one small little girl crawling around in the grass, but I didn't
want to slap her. I drifted away and walked around the block. When
I came back they were sitting on the ground in a straight line. The
first one would start to howl, then the second one, and so on down
the line, each taking their turn. I went and started to sit at
the end of the line, but the man said, "No, no, I'm the last. So
you can't sit here. This is my place." I looked down the line and
realized that everybody was attached to their exact position. I
looked around for Maxwell. I was so confused. Why was I required

to be here when I didn't fit into anything. I saw the little girl still crawling in the grass. I went over and sat down beside her. "What are you?" I said. "I'm a snake and I'm going to bite you," she said. "Bite me and get it over with," I said. So she crawled up to me and bit me on the leg. It hurt. "You're going to die now," she said. "I figured as much," I said. The howling had stopped. I turned around. They were taking turns diving through hoops of fire. I decided I didn't want to belong to the human race so I started making snakelike movements in the grass. Suddenly Maxwell was standing there. "You've failed this whole thing. I tried to tell you what to expect and look at you," he said. "I'm a snake," I said. "You're a very poor snake," he said.

To Advance No Farther into the Rubble of the Building

When I was in the grocery store a man came up to me and said,
"My, I admire your hat. Do you mind if I ask you where you got it?"
"I was in the Polish Army. I got it there," I said. "Well, I was
in the Polish Army, too. May I ask what regiment you were in?"
he said. "I was in the 172nd Regiment, infantry," I said. "That's
exactly what I was in. I never saw any hat like that," he said.
"Well, I'm sorry for you. Maybe you were sick or sleeping or away
on leave the day they handed out these hats. But, you're right,
it is a fine hat, keeps you warm in all kinds of weather," I said.
"I want that hat," he said, reaching for it. I grabbed his arm and
twisted it. "You're hurting me," he said. "Don't ever reach for
this hat again or I'll break your arm next time," I said. He looked
frightened and backed away from me. I threw some potatoes into
my basket and moved on. A little while later a woman came up to
me and said, "I just want to touch your hat. You saved my village.
I think I even remember your face. You were so brave in the face
of such a fierce enemy. You should let me buy you a bottle of the
best champagne." "I don't think we saved anything. We were really
outnumbered and outgunned," I said. "No, that's not true. You
were so brave and courageous," she said. "That was a long time
ago. I have forgotten many of the details," I said, and tried to
push past her. I was at the meat counter, studying the pork chops.
"I'll have those two fat ones," I told the man. "Are you Brownie
Kaczenski?" he said. "No, but I knew Brownie many years ago. He
was killed in the war," I said. "Oh, that's too bad. I grew up
with Brownie, and I lost track of him after he joined the army.
You look just like him, or what I thought he would have looked like
if he had survived. I'm sorry to hear about Brownie, but glad

you made it out alive. My family just barely got out," he said. He handed me my pork chops. I picked out some bread and cheese and was about to head for the checkout counter when a man pushed his cart in front of mine and said, "I ought to break your neck right here in front of everybody, you low-down, vicious killer. You killed my brother. I'd never forget your face." "I never killed anybody. I was on the run for most of the war. You've got the wrong man," I said. "You're a liar. I remember your face. I was just a little kid crouching behind the barn, but I know what I saw and it was you," he said. "You're mistaken, mister. I had a brother who was in the war and we looked a lot alike, but he was killed, too, just like your brother. I'm sorry, but it wasn't me I can assure you," I said. "Okay, killer, go on, but don't let me ever catch you in a dark alley," he said. I went up to the checkout counter and paid for my groceries. The clerk kept staring at me. "Is there something wrong?" I said. "It's the hat," he said. "Did you get it around here?" "No, I was in the Polish Army," I said. "Oh, cool," he said.

The Ice Cream Man

I answered the ad in the paper. I had been unemployed for
nine months and was desperate. At the interview, the man said,
"Do you have much experience climbing tall mountains?" "Absolutely.
I climb them all the time. If I see a tall mountain, I have to
climb it immediately," I said. "What about swimming long distances
in rough ocean waters, perhaps in a storm?" he said. "I'm like
a fish, you can't stop me. I just keep going in all kinds of
weather," I said. "Could you fly a glider at night and land in
a wheat field, possibly under enemy fire?" he said. "Nothing
could come more naturally to me," I said. "How are you with
explosives? Would a large building, say, twenty stories high
present you with much difficulty?" he said. "Certainly not. I
pride myself on a certain expertise," I said. "And I take it you
are fully acquainted with the latest in rocket launchers and land
mines?" he said. "I even own a few myself for personal use. They're
definitely no problem for me," I said. "Now, Mr. Strafford, or may
I call you Stephen, what you'll be doing is driving one of our ice
cream trucks, selling ice cream to all the little kids in the
neighborhood, but sometimes things get tricky and we like all our
drivers to be well-trained and well-equipped to face any eventu-
ality, you know, some fathers can get quite irate if you are out
of their kid's favorite flavor or if the kid drops the cone," he
said. "I understand, I won't hesitate to take appropriate action,"
I said. "And there are certain neighborhoods where you're under
advisement to expect the worst, sneak attacks, gang tactics,
bodies dropping from trees or rising out of manholes, blockades,
machine gun fire, launched explosives, flamethrowers and that kind
of thing. You can still do a little business there if you are on

your toes. Do you see what I'm saying?" he said. "No problem. I
know those kinds of neighborhoods, but, as you say, kids still want
their ice cream and I won't let them down," I said. "Good, Stephen,
I think you're going to like this job. It's exciting and challenging.
We've, of course, lost a few drivers over the years, but mostly it
was because they weren't paying attention. It's what I call the Santa
Claus complex. They thought they were there just to make the kids
happy. But there's a lot more to it than that. One of our best
drivers had to level half the city once. Of course, that was an
extreme case, but he did what needed to be done. We'll count on you
to be able to make that kind of decision. You'll have to have all
your weapons loaded and ready to go in a moment's notice. You'll
have your escape plans with you at all times," he said. "Yes, sir,
I'll be ready at all times," I said. "And, as you know, some of
the ice cream is lethal, so that will require a quick judgment call
on your part as well. Mistakes will inevitably be made, but try
to keep them at a minimum, otherwise the front office becomes
flooded with paperwork," he said. "I can assure you I will use it
only when I deem it absolutely necessary," I said. "Well, Stephen,
I look forward to your joining our team. They're mostly crack
professionals, ex–Green Berets and Navy Seals and that kind of
thing. At the end of the day you've made all those kids happy,
but you've also thinned out the bad seeds and made our city a
safer place to be," he said. He sat there smiling with immense
pride. "How will I know which flavor is lethal?" I said. "Experiment,"
he said. I looked stunned, then we both started laughing.

The Cowboy

Someone had spread an elaborate rumor about me, that I was
in possession of an extraterrestrial being, and I thought I knew who
it was. It was Roger Lawson. Roger was a practical joker of the
worst sort, and up till now I had not been one of his victims, so
I kind of knew my time had come. People parked in front of my
house for hours and took pictures. I had to draw all my blinds
and only went out when I had to. Then there was a barrage of
questions. "What does he look like?" "What do you feed him?" "How
did you capture him?" And I simply denied the presence of an
extraterrestrial in my house. And, of course, this excited them
all the more. The press showed up and started creeping around
my yard. It got to be very irritating. More and more came and
parked up and down the street. Roger was really working overtime
on this one. I had to do something. Finally, I made an announcement.
I said, "The little fellow died peacefully in his sleep at 11:02
last night." "Let us see the body," they clamored. "He went up
in smoke instantly," I said. "I don't believe you," one of them
said. "There is no body in the house or I would have buried it
myself," I said. About half of them got in their cars and drove
off. The rest of them kept their vigil, but more solemnly now.
I went out and bought some groceries. When I came back about an
hour later another half of them had gone. When I went into the kitchen
I nearly dropped the groceries. There was a nearly transparent
fellow with large pink eyes standing about three feet tall. "Why
did you tell them I was dead? That was a lie," he said. "You
speak English," I said. "I listen to the radio. It wasn't very
hard to learn. Also we have television. We get all your channels.
I like cowboys, especially John Ford movies. They're the best,"

he said. "What am I going to do with you?" I said. "Take me
to meet a real cowboy. That would make me happy," he said. "I
don't know any real cowboys, but maybe we could find one. But
people will go crazy if they see you. We'd have press following
us everywhere. It would be the story of the century," I said.
"I can be invisible. It's not hard for me to do," he said.
"I'll think about it. Wyoming or Montana would be our best bet, but
they're a long way from here," I said. "Please, I won't cause
you any trouble," he said. "It would take some planning," I said.
I put the groceries down and started putting them away. I tried
not to think of the cosmic meaning of all this. Instead, I
treated him like a smart little kid. "Do you have any sarsaparilla?"
he said. "No, but I have some orange juice. It's good for you,"
I said. He drank it and made a face. "I'm going to get the maps
out," I said. "We'll see how we could get there." When I came
back he was dancing on the kitchen table, a sort of ballet, but
very sad. "I have the maps," I said. "We won't need them. I just
received word. I'm going to die tonight. It's really a joyous
occasion, and I hope you'll help me celebrate by watching *The
Magnificent Seven*," he said. I stood there with the maps in my
hand. I felt an unbearable sadness come over me. "Why must
you die?" I said. "Father decides these things. It is probably
my reward for coming here safely and meeting you," he said. "But
I was going to take you to meet a real cowboy," I said. "Let's
pretend you are my cowboy," he said.

The Land of the Vapors

A rocket landed in a farmer's field just outside of town.
It didn't explode or anything, just stuck straight down in a
cow pasture. Word got out right away and a crowd started to
gather. Shortly after that the state police arrived and forced
everyone back to a safe distance. The farmer made sure all
his cows were in the barn. Then several army trucks arrived
and sent in several experts to look at the rocket. They were
covered in all manner of protective gear. The rest of the soldiers
assisted in keeping the crowd at a safe distance. I spotted Kim
and walked up to her. "This is quite embarrassing, isn't it?"
I said. "I'm not sure I want these people protecting us," she
said. "This isn't the first time this has happened around here,"
I said. "I know. There was that schoolhouse a couple of years
ago," she said. One of the soldiers turned around. "I wish
you wouldn't be so hard on us. We're still trying to get used
to the new system," he said. He looked so sad I almost forgave
him. "Well, couldn't you experiment with it out in the desert
or something," I said. "They did. They said everything was working
fine," he said. "Well, one of these days you're going to blow up
our whole little town and everybody in it. Do you really think
that's okay?" I said. "No, sir, I don't," he said. "It's not his
fault," Kim said to me. "I know, I know," I said. Just then
there was a tremendous explosion. Most of the crowd, including
the soldiers and policemen, had been knocked to the ground, some
of them bleeding. Some injured quite badly. The two soldiers
who had been working on the rocket had vaporized, not a trace of
them. And the barn had been flattened, a few of the cows still
standing. The farmer ran to the barn and started caressing

his decimated herd. I helped Kim to her feet. She had a cut above her left eye. The soldier who we'd been talking to was unconscious or possibly dead. I felt his pulse. He was still alive. "He'll be all right soon, I think," I said to Kim. I gave her my hand-kerchief. "Here, hold this over your eye." We started to walk among the others. "The ambulances will be here soon," I kept saying over and over to those who needed help. I knelt down to one old lady and helped her find her rosary. She thanked me and smiled. I gave sips of water to a young boy with parched lips. Finally, the ambulances did arrive and started carting away the wounded. One police officer said to me, "They train us for this kind of thing, but it never does any good. A goddamned field of cows, who could have expected that." "Yeah, that farmer lost half his herd and his barn, nobody's going to care about that," I said. "I wasn't thinking about that. I was thinking about what a waste of a good missile," he said. Kim and I drove back to town. "Do you want me to take you to the hospital so you can get that eye stitched up?" I said. "No, I'll be all right," she said. "I'm not going to go chasing missiles again. That was a mistake," I said. "Oh, don't say that, Brad. You know it's the most exciting thing that ever happens around here. If it weren't for the army this would be a very dull little town. As it is, it's almost as if we were at war, but with ourselves, which puts a whole other spin on things. You don't really have to hate anybody, which is a big relief," she said. "But what about those two men who were vaporized?" I said. "That was their calling. They went happily to the land of the vapors," she said.

The Quota

I tell myself that I'm waiting around for some kind of
enlightenment, but nothing really ever happens. I take the
dog for a walk. He chases some squirrels. He looks like he's
going to get into a fight with another dog, but they end up rolling
around in the grass having a great time. I think there must be
a lesson there. Back home, I find I have been selected for jury
duty. I think, but I'm insane, I'm deaf, I'm blind. I'm the last
person they would ever want. I put on a pot of coffee and settle
down in the living room with a magazine. There's a story of an
elderly widow who lives with her six-hundred-pound pig. She says
that pig would protect her against any intruder. She says it has
already scared off three, maiming one of them almost beyond
recognition. She also says it is a very tidy and affectionate pig.
I have to think about this a long time. I pour myself a cup of
coffee. I think that woman is lying about something, though I've
found that most bizarre stories have some truth in them. The phone
rings. It's Maurice. He says, "Rudy, I need to talk to you. It's
a matter of the utmost importance. When would it be convenient for
me to come over?" I say, "Maurice, you didn't even ask me how I
was. Where are your manners, for chrissake?" "Rudy, forgive me,
it's just that this thing can't wait, and I don't think it's right
to discuss it on the phone," he said. "You still didn't ask me
how I was. Oh, well, forget it. You never have been all that polite,"
I said. "Can I come right now," he said. "How about a week from
today, say, at noon," I said. "But, Rudy, this is urgent," he said.
"Okay, come on over, but this better be good, because you're interrupting
my experiments," I said. Fifteen minutes later Maurice was at the
door. "What is it?" I said. "Lance is in jail, and they've picked

up Alfred and Felix as well," he said. "What are they charged with?" I said. "Suspected terrorist activities," he said. "Well, that's crazy," I said. "I know, but I fear we'll be next," he said. "I've never done anything, well, there was that bottle rocket, but I don't see how that could count," I said. "It doesn't matter. They've got their quota to fill and they're desperate," he said. "What are you going to do?" I said. "Well, I'm thinking about leaving the country. I've got an uncle in Hong Kong who's promised me a job in a bank. He runs the bank. He could probably get you a job, too," he said. "No, thanks. I've read an article about Hong Kong in *National Geographic*. I don't think it's for me, and I can't picture myself as a banker," I said. "It beats a long prison sentence," he said. "I'm sure something will work out for the best," I said. "Well, okay, Rudy, I just thought you should know. You seem quite content here in your bubble, so I won't disturb you any longer," he said. We shook hands and he left. The article also said that the pig could count to ten. I thought about all that Maurice had told me. It's true, we live in restless, unpredictable times, but you still have to go on being a human being with all the hopes and dreams you ever had, or what's the use? I strive for enlightenment, but what is that, really? A peek through the cracks of the castle wall? A carrot is just a carrot, and a man is just a man waiting for the next thing to happen. But a pig that can count to ten is a thing of glory.

Billy

Nothing could be better than a Sunday afternoon at the
ballpark. However, since that is not in the range of my activities,
I would not be the one who said that. It is that man over there
in the ball cap and loud Hawaiian shirt. I walk up to him and
say, "That was a contemptible, asinine thing you just said."
He grabs my neck and shouts into my face, "Nothing could be better
than a Sunday afternoon at the ballpark!" "Well, yes," I said.
"That is a most pleasant place to be. You can't beat it for sheer
pleasure." He dropped me to the ground and said, "If you dare to
mock me I'll kick you to the moon." I rolled into a little ball
and whimpered. He walked away, glancing over his shoulder several
times. People gathered around me. "What is that?" somebody said.
"It looks like the wasted husk of a human being," a woman said.
"Somebody should sweep it up," a man said. I unrolled myself and
stood up. "My name's Billy," I said. "I was just resting after
a long day. My job's very demanding." They all walked away with-
out a word. It was still early. All the shops were open. Two
men walked by. One of them said, "Nothing could be better than
a Sunday afternoon at the ballpark." I said, "Somebody else has
already said that." He stopped and looked at me. "Oh, yeah, what
does that make me, a parrot? Do I look like a parrot to you?" he
said. "Maybe a slight resemblance," I said. "You think you're
some kind of comedian, don't you?" he said. He came over and grabbed
me by the neck and lifted me off the ground. "You're hurting me,"
I said. He threw me against the building and I slid to the ground.
The two men walked on, continuing their conversation. I resisted
the urge to curl up into a ball. Instead, I struggled to stand up,
and when I did I brushed myself off and took a couple of steps.

Then I started walking with a real sense of purpose. People stared at me as if I were a lunatic escaped from lockup, or maybe they were envious of what I had. I heard that thing said again about Sunday afternoon at the ballpark, but this time I just ignored it. I thought there must be a disease going around. I felt sorry for them. I stopped at the funeral home and watched the pallbearers carry the casket to the limo. I turned around and started running. Finally, I found the man who said it. I grabbed his arm and said, "You've got a disease. It's going to kill you. You have to go to a doctor right now. Trust me, I know what I'm talking about." "You're crazy. Let go of my arm," he said. "It's going to eat your brain up. It's very unpleasant. No more Sundays at the ballpark for you," I said. He walked away, extremely annoyed. I stood under a paulownia tree, its panicles of fragrant violet flowers almost smothering.

The March

There were two or three stragglers who couldn't keep up
with the rest. I said to the captain, "What should we do about
the stragglers?" He said, "Shoot them. Stragglers are often
captured by the enemy and tortured until they reveal our where-
abouts. It is best to not leave them behind." I went back to
the stragglers and told them that my orders were to shoot them.
They started running to catch up with the rest. Then a sniper
was shot out of a tree. "Good work," said the captain. Then
we climbed a mountain. Once we were on top, the captain said,
"I'll give a hundred dollars to anyone who can spot the enemy."
Nobody could. "We'll spend the night here," the captain said.
I was appointed first lookout. I smoked a cigarette and looked
into the forest below through my night-vision glasses. Something
moved, but it was hard to tell what it was. There was a lot of
movement, but it didn't seem like men, more like animals. I soon
fell asleep. When Juarez tapped me on the shoulder to tell me he
would take over, he said, "You were asleep, weren't you?" I
stared at him with pleading eyes. "The captain would have you
shot, you know?" I didn't say anything. The next morning Juarez
was missing. "Captain, do you want me to send out a search party?"
I said. "No, I always suspected he was with the enemy," he said.
"Today, we will descend the mountain." "Yes, sir, Captain," I
said. The men tumbled and rolled, bounced up against trees and
boulders. Some of them broke their arms and noses. I was standing
next to the captain at the bottom of the mountain. "Shoot them
all!" he ordered. "But, Captain, they're our men," I said. "No
they're not. My men were well-trained and disciplined. Look
at this mess here. They are not my men. Shoot them!" he again

ordered. I raised my rifle, then turned and smacked him in the head with the butt of it. Then I knelt and handcuffed him. The soldiers gathered about me and we headed for home. Of course, none of us knew where that was, but we had our dreams and our memories. Or I think we did.

The War Next Door

I thought I saw some victims of the last war bandaged and
limping through the forest beside my house. I thought I recognized
some of them, but I wasn't sure. It was kind of a hazy dream
from which I tried to wake myself, but they were still there,
bloody, some of them on crutches, some lacking limbs. This sad
parade went on for hours. I couldn't leave the window. Finally,
I opened the door. "Where are you going?" I shouted. "We're
just trying to escape," one of them shouted back. "But the war's
over," I said. "No it's not," one said. All the news reports had
said it had been over for days. I didn't know who to trust. It's
best to just ignore them, I told myself. They'll go away. So I
went into the living room and picked up a magazine. There was a
picture of a dead man. He had just passed my house. And another
dead man I recognized. I ran back in the kitchen and looked out.
A group of them were headed my way. I opened the door. "Why
didn't you fight with us?" they said. "I didn't know who the
enemy was, honest, I didn't," I said. "That's a fine answer. I
never did figure it out myself," one of them said. The others looked
at him as if he were crazy. "The other side was the enemy, obviously,
the ones with the beady eyes," said another. "They were mean,"
another said, "terrible." "One was very kind to me, cradled me
in his arms," said one. "Well, you're all dead now. A lot of
good that will do you," I said. "We're just gaining our strength
back," one of them said. I shut the door and went back in the
living room. I heard scratches at the window at first, but then
they faded off. I heard a bugle in the distance, then the roar of
a cannon. I still didn't know which side I was on.